## Praise for The Coun[

"A sparkling comedy of errors tuc
loved it!"

— Susan M. Boyer,
*USA Today* Bestselling Author of *Lowcountry Book Club*

"Readers who enjoy the novels of Susan Isaacs will love this series that blends a strong mystery with the demands of living in an exclusive society."

— *Kings River Life Magazine*

"From the first page to the last, Julie's mysteries grab the reader and don't let up."

— Sally Berneathy,
*USA Today* Bestselling Author of *The Ex Who Saw a Ghost*

"This book is fun! F-U-N Fun!...A delightful pleasure to read. I didn't want to put it down...Highly recommend."

— *Mysteries, etc.*

"Set in Kansas City, Missouri, in 1974, this cozy mystery effectively recreates the era through the details of down-to-earth Ellison's everyday life."

— *Booklist*

"Mulhern's lively, witty sequel to *The Deep End* finds Kansas City, Mo., socialite Ellison Russell reluctantly attending a high school football game...Cozy fans will eagerly await Ellison's further adventures."

— *Publishers Weekly*

"There's no way a lover of suspense could turn this book down because it's that much fun."

— *Suspense Magazine*

"Cleverly written with sharp wit and all the twists and turns of the best '70s primetime drama, Mulhern nails the fierce fraught mother-daughter relationship, fearlessly tackles what hides behind the Country Club façade, and serves up justice in bombshell fashion. A truly satisfying slightly twisted cozy."

– Gretchen Archer,
*USA Today* Bestselling Author of *Double Knot*

"Part mystery, part women's fiction, part poetry, Mulhern's debut, *The Deep End*, will draw you in with the first sentence and entrance you until the last. An engaging whodunit that kept me guessing until the end!"

– Tracy Weber,
Author of the Downward Dog Mysteries

"An impossible-to-put-down Harvey Wallbanger of a mystery. With a smart, funny protagonist who's learning to own her power as a woman, *Send in the Clowns* is one boss read."

– Ellen Byron,
Agatha Award-Nominated Author of *Plantation Shudders*

"The plot is well-structured and the characters drawn with a deft hand. Setting the story in the mid-1970s is an inspired touch...A fine start to this mystery series, one that is highly recommended."

– *Mysterious Reviews*

"What a fun read! Murder in the days before cell phones, the internet, DNA and AFIS."

– *Books for Avid Readers*

# WATCHING THE DETECTIVES

**The Country Club Murders**
**by Julie Mulhern**

# WATCHING THE DETECTIVES

## THE COUNTRY CLUB MURDERS

HENERY PRESS

WATCHING THE DETECTIVES
The Country Club Murders
Part of the Henery Press Mystery Collection

First Edition | May 2017

Henery Press
www.henerypress.com

Trade Paperback ISBN-13: 978-1-63511-211-5
Digital epub ISBN-13: 978-1-63511-212-2
Kindle ISBN-13: 978-1-63511-213-9
Hardcover ISBN-13: 978-1-63511-214-6

Printed in the United States of America

*For my family. Love to you all.*

## ACKNOWLEDGMENTS

My thanks to Madonna and Sally for all they do, to my family for putting up with deadlines and me talking about murder in restaurants, to the best proofer ever, and to my editors Erin, Kendel, and Rachel. It takes a village.

# ONE

There were Mondays—burnt toast, no cream for the coffee, a body in the swimming pool—and there were Mondays.

This was one of *those* Mondays.

The morning began auspiciously enough—golden toast, plenty of cream, no bodies—but it went sideways quickly.

How was I to know when I heard the doorbell ring that I should have stayed in bed?

On the stoop stood a woman I wasn't entirely sure I wanted in my home. Nonetheless, I smiled and opened the door wide. "Khaki, welcome. Please, come in."

My last decorator wore Ferragamo flats and twin sets. She also tried to sell me stolen art.

This decorator shod her feet in stacked heel boots the exact shade of Dijon mustard. She paired those groovy boots with a short suede skirt and a sweater with a scooped neckline that revealed a startling amount of cleavage.

Why wear such an outfit to an appointment with me? I would not be swayed by the deep vee of her sweater. Was it a visual reminder that she was younger, hipper, and sexier? A not-so-subtle signal that if she couldn't hold her ex-husband's interest, I had no hope?

I forced a smile. Hunter Tafft had done so much for me, I could hardly say no when he asked me to allow his ex-wife to submit a proposal for redoing the study. Looking at her, definitely younger, hipper, and sexier, I regretted my lack of gumption.

Khaki stepped into the foyer and her gaze took in the bombe

chest topped with a crystal vase filled with bronze mums, the sweeping staircase that led to the second floor, the rugs, the art, the crown moldings, and the color of the walls. "You have a lovely home."

"Thank you. Would you care for coffee?"

She wrinkled her nose. "I never touch the stuff."

She didn't drink coffee? That hardly seemed trustworthy. I liked her less and less. "Tea?"

"No, thank you."

Probably just as well. There was no telling the age of the Lipton tea bags at the back of the cupboard. We smiled at each other. Politely. Strangers who'd decided to make the best of an uncomfortable situation—as uncomfortable as Shetland wool against bare skin.

"The study is this way." I led her to my late husband's den. Heavy drapes, dark paneling, a mahogany desk the size of Rhode Island, leather furniture, hideous shag carpet, and the lingering scent of tobacco made the room feel like a cave—or given that it was Henry's room, a well-appointed dungeon.

"Oh my." She dug in her purse and removed a steno pad and pen. "What did you have in mind?"

"Something lighter."

She nodded. "Does the paneling stay?"

"Yes."

"Hunter doesn't care for paneling."

*Hunter doesn't live here.* Hunter Tafft was devastatingly handsome, terminally charming, thrice divorced, and the man Mother had selected to be my next husband. If I had my numbers right, Khaki was his second wife.

"He's very particular," she added

The muscles in my back and shoulders tightened. This was not a suitable conversation. This was exactly what I'd worried about when I called her.

"Although—" she rubbed her chin "—given your successful career, he may not be as picky."

Did she have any idea how wildly inappropriate her remarks were? Apparently not. Her lips curled, pleased with the knowledge that she possessed secrets to Hunter Tafft that I did not.

"I've often thought that if I'd had a career we'd still be together. He likes independent women—or he thinks he does." She finished the last bit with a tight little smile.

*Brngg, brngg.*

I thanked God for the interruption and lunged for the phone. "Hello."

"Bess is dead."

I tightened my hold on the receiver. "You're sure?"

"I—" Aggie's voice cracked. "I'm sure."

"I'm so sorry." And I was. Aggie, my housekeeper, loved Bess with singular devotion. Bess dead? Aggie without her rattletrap Bug would be like Sonny without Cher or MacMillan without Wife. Mother would be thrilled by the news. Mother thought Bess was as out of place at my house as white shoes after Labor Day.

"Where are you?" I asked. "I'll come get you."

Khaki raised her brows.

"Milgrim's." Aggie's voice frayed at the edges.

"You've been marketing?"

"I have four bags." Her words sounded wet, tear-soaked.

"I'm on my way." I hung up the phone. "Khaki, I apologize, but I'm going to have to run out for a few minutes. Will you be all right on your own?"

Khaki frowned. "Is everything okay?" She sounded as if she cared.

"My housekeeper has car trouble."

Her face cleared. "Go." She dug a Polaroid camera out of her cavernous handbag, put it on the desk, and stuck her hand in the bag a second time. She dug—and dug. Her brows drew together. "Aha!" Her face cleared and she pulled out a tape measure. "I'll take a few more measurements. If I get done before you get back, I'll lock up."

"Thank you." Maybe Khaki wasn't so bad after all. Or maybe I was just grateful to get away from her Shetland wool scratchiness. She could offer the lowest bid in the history of low bids, but I wouldn't hire her. Being around her was too awkward.

I grabbed my purse, dashed out the front door, jumped in my Triumph, and prayed there was enough room in the trunk for four grocery bags.

The drive to the market was short and Aggie was easy to spot. She was the only redhead wearing a sky-blue muumuu mourning over a VW Beetle held together with chicken wire and love.

A woman stood next to her—a pretty blonde with a sympathetic tilt to her head. Mary Beth Brewer. A genuinely nice woman. If anyone other than me was going to watch over Bess with Aggie, Mary Beth was a good choice.

Aggie's usual pep had disappeared. Her sproingy hair drooped. As did her eyes and the corners of her mouth. Even her muumuu looked ready to cry.

I climbed out of my car and eyed Bess. "I'm so sorry. I know a good mechanic." I drove a Triumph. Knowing a good mechanic was a necessity.

"I think she's past the mechanic stage." Aggie patted Bess's roof. A tear formed at the corner of her eye and ran unchecked down her cheek. "My husband gave her to me for my birthday in 1960." She didn't add that losing Bess was like losing Al all over again. She didn't have to.

I searched for something to say, found nothing, and hugged her.

A moment passed and she pulled away. "We should—" she wiped her eyes with the back of her hand "—we should get these groceries home. The ice cream is melting."

"I offered to drive her." Mary Beth shifted her doubtful gaze between Aggie's four bags of groceries and my tiny car.

"Thank you," I said. "That was kind, but we'll manage."

Somehow we crammed the shopping bags into the Triumph's tiny trunk. Well, three of them. Aggie held the fourth on her lap.

We didn't talk about calling a tow service, or buying a new car, or the unexpected warmth of the November afternoon—so warm we left the top down. Instead, we drove in a respectful silence. Presumably Aggie relived her years with Bess. I worried that I'd left Max, the dastardly dog who plots to take over my house, alone in the backyard.

Unsupervised, he might dig his way to China or, worse, into my neighbor Margaret Hamilton's yard.

I drove faster.

We pulled into the circle drive and parked behind Khaki's BMW.

"Who's here?" Aggie asked.

"The decorator. I thought she'd be done by now." I got out of the car, opened the trunk, and pulled out a bag.

Together, Aggie and I walked up the front steps.

The door wasn't quite closed.

I carried my bag of groceries to the kitchen and deposited it on the counter then walked toward Henry's study. "Khaki?"

No answer.

"Khaki?" My voice rose.

I pushed open the door.

Khaki lay on Henry's heinous carpet and stared at the ceiling.

Well, not stared. She wasn't actually looking at anything. Not with a bullet hole between her eyes.

Oh dear Lord.

It wasn't possible.

It was all too possible. I dropped my purse on the floor and covered my heart with my hands, hoping they might somehow keep it in my chest.

I joined Khaki on the floor. I had to—my knees gave out. Four days. Four. Days. That's all the time that had passed since a demented clown tried to kill me. Now this?

Mother was going to have a stroke.

Given my heart rate, I might join her.

"Aggie!" Her name came out as a strangled yelp.

The knock of her clogs on the hardwood reached me before she did. Max was coming too—his nails clicked against the wood floor. I waited for them, leaning against a chest of drawers near the door. Stars sparkled around my head.

"What's wrong?" Aggie entered the study and stumbled. "Oh, hell."

That was an understatement.

We both gazed at poor Khaki. Max, too. He sat, cocked his head, and stared first at the body and then at me as if to say *another one?*

A handle poked me in the back and I shifted. "Would you please help me up?" I didn't exactly trust my legs.

Aggie hauled me off the floor. "We need to get out of the house."

"We need to call the police."

She glanced over her shoulder as if she expected a killer to leap out at us. "Not from here." She grasped my elbow and led me to the front door. "Stay here. I'll get Max's leash."

Max's ears perked. *Leash* meant walk. Not hardly.

Aggie was overreacting. If there was a murderer in the house, Max wouldn't trot after Aggie as if we were preparing for a grand adventure, he'd have the culprit cornered in a closet. But finding Khaki had rendered me near mute. I didn't have the energy for an argument.

With Max straining at the end of a leash, Aggie joined me on the front stoop. Where to go? My nice next-door neighbor was ill. The other was a bona fide witch. Disturbing either of them was a bad idea.

"Let's go across the street." I pointed at a stately Tudor. "We can call from the Dixons'."

A moment later, I rang their bell. Marian Dixon came to the door. She glanced at me then Aggie then Max. "Ellison, what's wrong?"

"Marian, may I please use your phone?"

She stared at Max, apparently frozen.

"I wouldn't ask if it wasn't important."

"Of course." She beckoned us into her home.

We stepped inside and stopped cold.

Marian, whom I'd always considered a sane woman, had taken a slight detour into crazy town.

Aggie, Max, and I were surrounded by a veritable flock of owls. There was a latch hook rug hung on the wall which featured no less than five owls lined on a branch, an owl lamp sat on a narrow table, and a Hickory chair with an owl instead of a harp as its back sat next to it. An owl plant stand held a Boston fern and an owl umbrella stand held owl decorated umbrellas.

Thank God she didn't seem to expect me to comment. All those owls rendered me speechless.

"This way." Marian led us through an owl infested living room into a sun porch where macramé owls in various colors perched on the wall. "Do you need a phone book?"

I found my tongue. "No, thank you. I know the number."

"I'm going to make some coffee. You look as if you could use a cup." She might be crazier than a barn owl, but Marian Dixon was a good woman.

"Thank you." I picked up the phone and dialed Detective Anarchy Jones' number. Both Mother and my daughter, Grace, call him "my" detective. They use different tones when they say it. Mother does not approve of my burgeoning relationship with a cop. Grace thinks he's handsome and slightly dangerous. Grace is right.

He answered on the third ring. "Jones."

"Anarchy—" Why was my mouth suddenly dry? "—it's Ellison."

"Who's dead?"

He meant it to be funny. I'm sure he did. But the thought of Khaki staring sightlessly at the ceiling of my late husband's study was too much. My throat closed. My eyes watered. My ability to speak went the way of the dodo bird. I handed the phone to Aggie.

"Detective Jones," she said. "This is Aggie DeLucci, Mrs. Russell's housekeeper. There's a dead body in the study." She listened for a moment, a sour expression settling onto her face. "It's Mrs. Russell's decorator and she's been shot."

She fell silent.

"Across the street at the Dixons'." More listening then she hung up the phone. "He does not, under any circumstances, want us to go back to the house."

I nodded my agreement. "I need to call Mother anyway." God forbid she heard about another murder from the neighbors. I dialed.

The phone rang the requisite three rings. "Hello." Mother answered the phone herself.

"It's me."

"I'm glad you called. I want you to sponsor a luncheon. You must buy a table."

"There's a problem."

"No, there's not. Donate the table if you can't come." Mother would probably prefer that. My recent track record with events wasn't stellar. "Cora needs all the help she can get."

Poor Cora. I could hear the curl in Mother's lip when she said her name. Disdain was too nice a word for what Mother thought of her cousin's wife. Why was she helping?

"Thornton sees a disaster in the making and asked me to step in."

It was as if Mother could read my mind. As for Mother's mind, it remained a mystery. And as to why Mother adored her domineering first cousin—that mystery ranked up there with what happened to DB Cooper.

"They have a national speaker coming."

"Fine. I'll buy a table. There's something—"

"You might enjoy the talk—"

"Mother!"

"What?"

"It's about Khaki White. She—"

Mother tsked. Loudly. She probably couldn't help it. "You told me. She came over to your house this morning. She's redoing your study."

Not much chance of that now. "She was bidding the job."

"Was? You decided on someone else?" I could *hear* Mother's smile through the phone line. "It's probably for the best. I realize Hunter recommended her, but I've heard a few things about her. Shady things. Do you know the divorce rate among her clients?"

"No. It doesn't matter. I'm not married and—"

"But you could be." She meant to Hunter. Silver-haired, silver-tongued, successful lawyer—practically perfect in every way.

"I've been widowed for less than six months." Of course, Henry's and my marriage was over long before he died, but Mother believed in the niceties. Remarrying within a year of Henry's death would be unseemly.

"He won't wait forever, Ellison. You can't let the grass grow." She paused, presumably to give me time to worry that Hunter Tafft might slip through my clumsy fingers. "As far as decorators go, everyone is using Anne Callison and—"

"Mother!"

"What, dear? You do realize it's impolite to interrupt?"

I pinched the bridge of my nose. "Khaki is dead."

"Well, at least you won't have to fire her. I know firing Priscilla couldn't have been easy, but after that mess with the Chinese screens, you didn't have much choice—" Mother was babbling and Mother was not a babbler. She was more of a steamroll-you-with-the-force-of-her-words-er. "—and really, Anne is who you want—"

Enough. "Khaki is dead in Henry's study."

"You don't mean…" The babbling brook of her tone froze solid. Walk-without-fear-of-breaking-through-the-ice froze solid.

"Khaki was murdered." There. I'd told her. Now I waited…Ten. Nine. Eight. Seven.

She exploded. "Ellison, this simply must stop. Do you have any idea how—"

Four seconds to make Khaki's death my fault. It had to be a new record. "Mother, I have to go. I'll talk to you later. Goodbye." I hung up the phone.

"She's not happy?" Aggie paired her question with a sympathetic smile.

Max whined softly.

"No. She's not." An understatement of epic proportions. I picked up the phone and dialed yet another number. "Hunter Tafft, please."

"I'm sorry, Mr. Tafft is in a meeting." The voice on the other end of the line was cool and professional.

"This is an emergency."

"I'll be happy to take a message." Still cool but bordering on frosty.

"I need to speak with Mr. Tafft immediately."

"I'm sorry, Mr. Tafft cannot be disturbed." Cooler yet. Not quite Mother's brook-frozen-solid tone, but close.

"Tell her it's duck club business," whispered Aggie.

"It's duck club business."

The cool, professional voice fell silent for a second. "I'll slip a note in front of him, ma'am. Who may I say is calling?"

"Ellison Russell."

"Please hold."

I stared at Marian's flock of macramé owls and drummed my fingers on a brass side table.

After a moment, Hunter said, "Ellison?"

"Hunter." My tongue stopped working. How does one tell a man his second ex-wife is dead? I held the phone out to Aggie. Twice now I'd chickened out. At least I'd faced Mother. Sort of.

Aggie offered me a sympathetic frown and took the receiver from my hands. "Mr. Tafft, it's Aggie."

She fell silent. Listened.

"No," she said. "There's been an incident."

Again she listened.

"Mrs. Russell is fine, but there's been a murder."

"What?" Hunter's bark positively boomed from the phone. "Who?"

"Mrs. White in the study with a revolver."

# TWO

One would think, with all the experience I'd had waiting for police, I'd be better at it.

One would be mistaken.

There were things that didn't improve with practice—finding bodies and waiting for homicide detectives being chief among them.

I paced the length of the Dixons' sunroom, glared at the owls (they glared back), and smiled at Marian when she appeared with coffee. "Thank you."

I accepted the mug (of course it was shaped like an owl) and took a small grateful sip. The coffee was not good. It wasn't even mediocre. In fact, the coffee (if that's what it actually was) tasted like tiny bits of burnt dirt against my tongue. My hostess needed an introduction to Mr. Coffee.

I choked down a second sip (Mother would be pleased with my manners—not that good manners mattered a whit to her now. Not in the face of my finding yet another body). "Marian, did you see anyone going in or out of my house this afternoon?"

"No. I saw you leave. Around noon I think it was." Her head settled into her shoulders like an owl's. "A few minutes later, when I looked out the window, there was a white Mercedes parked in the drive."

Now I knew who'd been keeping tabs on me—Mother's source for all things Ellison. Marian probably sat in this owl-infested room, watched everything that happened across the street, and reported it to Mother. Maybe I wouldn't introduce her to Mr. Coffee after all. Marian and the percolator-from-hell responsible for the cup of liquid masquerading as coffee could spend eternity together. Mr. Coffee and his magic would remain my secret.

Marian smoothed the plucked arch of her brow and donned a holier-than-thou expression. "I remember thinking it was odd because I knew you'd gone. I figured he was waiting for you to come home."

"Who?" Or, given Marian's macramé friends, *hoo?*

"Hunter Tafft."

My stomach plunged to my feet. My heart rose to my throat. Marian was wrong. She had to be wrong. Of course she was wrong.

"You saw Hunter Tafft across the street?" Aggie's voice was as sharp as a carving knife.

"His car was there." The holiest among holies expression remained fixed on Marian's face. She was not gossiping. She was merely sharing information.

Aggie was as protective of Hunter as a mother bear of her cubs. Hunter had helped Aggie's late husband through his final illness. "There are lots of white Mercedes."

My thought exactly.

"But only one that's regularly parked in Ellison's drive." Marian's tone suggested she didn't appreciate arguments from a housekeeper.

"Did you actually *see* Hunter?" I put a conciliatory note in my voice.

"No." The word was grudging, a reluctant admission. Marian crossed her arms, a study in obstinacy. "But I recognized the car. I'm sure it was his. He had to be there." She spoke with absolute assurance.

I sank onto the chaise lounge and let my head settle into the cradle of my hands. There was a dead woman in my study—God rest her soul—and that was not the worst part of this day. Marian Dixon was about to implicate Hunter in a murder based on the color of his car.

Detective Anarchy Jones had demonstrated his willingness to

throw Hunter Tafft in a suspect pool. Now he had a reason. A good one. I knew, with the same certainty that I knew macramé owls would never perch on my walls, that Hunter hadn't killed his ex-wife. Why would he? She'd remarried. He didn't even have to pay alimony.

I lifted my head. "Aggie, what time did you call me?"

"Around noon."

I glanced at my watch. The dial read just shy of one. "If I left the house around five after twelve, and we got back at 12:25, that means Khaki was killed in those twenty minutes."

"Yes." Aggie nodded.

Marian stared. All eyes. Like an owl.

I took another sip of God-awful coffee, suppressed a shudder, and put the cup down on a side table. "We just got off the phone with Hunter." We. Ha! Aggie had spoken with Hunter. "I don't see how he could be here between 12:05 and 12:25, then in his office when I called."

"Probably not." Why weren't the worry lines disappearing from Aggie's forehead?

"Also, it sounded as if he was in an important meeting."

Aggie shook her head. "That's doubtful. If he's working at his desk, he doesn't like being disturbed. Chances are good he was eating a tuna fish sandwich and reading a brief."

"But the receptionist handed him a note."

"She did. And the office isn't close." A few of the lines squinching Aggie's eyes together smoothed.

"He couldn't have done it."

"Like that will make a whit of difference to him." She jerked her chin toward the front window which offered a phenomenal view of Anarchy Jones climbing out of an unmarked police car parked in my driveway.

Anarchy glanced over his shoulder as if he could feel the weight of our gazes.

I rose to my feet and lifted my hand in a wave.

Marian, in an awed voice, asked, "Isn't that your detective?"

Aggie scowled.

Her scowl deepened when Anarchy walked toward the Dixons' rather than my front door.

Marian tittered and smoothed her hair.

I dropped my hand to my side. I was past the smoothing hair stage when it came to Anarchy. Maybe.

A second man got out of the car. One I didn't know. One who looked as if he'd borrowed Columbo's trench coat, rolled it in a ball, used it as a pillow for a week or two, then decided to wear it. He stared up at my house, hunched his shoulders, and shoved his hands in his pockets.

Anarchy strode across the street and up Marian's front walk.

Marian tittered again. "I'll get the door." She disappeared into the living room. A few seconds later the sound of voices in the foyer reached us.

A few seconds after that, Detective Anarchy Jones stood framed in the double doorway to Marian's sunroom. "Ellison." He stared at me with eyes the color of perfectly-brewed coffee. His was not an appraising ooh-la-la stare, more of a disaster-strikes-again-and-once-again-Ellison-is-in-the-thick-of-it stare. "Who is dead?"

I swallowed and refrained from smoothing my hair. "Khaki White."

He closed his eyes for an instant. "Who exactly is Khaki White?"

"The most expensive decorator in town." Marian sniffed. "She doesn't like owls."

Anarchy's eyes scanned the owl wall, the chaise, the precarious stack of books at its side, and the coffee mug on the side table. "May I please have a cup of coffee, Marian?"

Marian? They were on a first-name basis already?

"Of course." Marian practically shimmied with the joy of fulfilling his request. She hurried off to the kitchen.

"Who is Khaki White?" Anarchy repeated.

"The decorator I asked to give me a bid to redo the study."

His brows drew slightly together. "The study?"

"Henry's office." If I wanted to rename the rooms in my house, that was my prerogative.

"What happened?" Anarchy's brown eyes held his cop expression, serious and intense.

"Khaki was taking measurements when Aggie called."

"Measurements?"

"I'm going to replace the carpet."

He nodded. "Then what?"

"I left Khaki alone at the house. Aggie had car trouble and I went to get her. When we got home, Khaki was dead."

Anarchy pressed the index and middle finger of each hand against his temples. "You left her alone?"

"Yes."

"How long were you gone?"

"Twenty minutes. Tops."

"So, in twenty minutes, someone gained access to your house, killed Miss White, and left."

"It's Mrs."

"Pardon me?"

"It's Mrs." I glanced at Marian's wall of owls. They regarded me with smirks on their beaks. *That Ellison Russell, she's in a world of trouble. Again.* I shifted my gaze to the ceiling. I had to tell him. If I didn't, he'd find out and wonder why I hadn't. "Khaki was married to Stan White. Before that she was married to Hunter Tafft."

Next to me, Aggie exhaled. A sudden puff of breath that communicated very clearly she wouldn't have told Anarchy about Hunter and Khaki. At least not yet.

"You hired Tafft's ex-wife as a decorator?" He shook his head, unable to wrap his mind around the idea. "Why?"

"He asked me to. And I hadn't hired her. Not yet. I was just getting a bid."

"Why?"

"You'd have to ask him."

"No. Why did you ask her for a bid?"

"She's good. My last decorator—" I gazed up at the hard planes of his face "—you know what happened." A near-death run-in with a murderous clown. That's what.

There was a serious tilt to his strong chin. "Did Tafft know you'd asked Mrs. White to bid on your study?"

"Yes."

"Did he know she'd be at your house today?"

"I didn't tell him." I suppressed the urge to add, *cross my heart and hope to die.*

"Who knew she'd be at your house today?"

"Just my bridge group." And, by extension, possibly hundreds of people. That did not need to be explained.

"I'm sure Mrs. White didn't tell him." Aggie sounded confident. "They seldom spoke."

"Really?" Anarchy shifted his cop gaze to Aggie. "Then why did he recommend her to Ellison?"

"I have your coffee." Marian's voice was as bright as a new morning. Not *this* morning. *This* morning, despite perfect toast and plenty of cream, had given way to an afternoon that included a body. She extended the cup like an offering.

Anarchy accepted the cup. "Thank you." He drank and the line of his jaw tightened. Tepid, burnt brown water dotted with coffee grounds will do that to a man.

"I should have asked." Marian's slightly dazed expression hadn't changed. "Would you care for cream or sugar?"

As if either could mask the taste of her coffee. Straight scotch couldn't mask the taste of her coffee.

"No, thank you." Anarchy glanced again at the comfortable chaise and the stack of books. "This is a nice room. You must spend a great deal of time in here." His gaze shifted to the view of my house.

"I do." Marian was more eager to please than a Labrador puppy.

"Were you in here around lunchtime?"

"I was. I saw Ellison leaving. Then I went back to my book."

She nodded toward the novel on the top of the stack, *The Pirate* by Harold Robbins. "It's thrilling. You should read it." She gazed at Anarchy as if he were a billionaire wrapped in intrigue and not a police detective wrapped in an ugly sport coat.

"I'll put it on my list. Did you see anything else? Anyone going in or out of Mrs. Russell's house?"

Marian cut her gaze toward Aggie and me. "When I looked up again there was a white Mercedes in the drive."

"Oh?" Anarchy ought to work harder at keeping enthusiasm out of his voice. That *oh* was entirely too eager. "What time was that?"

"Around twelve fifteen."

"Did you see anyone?"

Marian's gaze, like a compass pointing toward true north, returned to Anarchy. "No, but the car belonged to Hunter Tafft."

As if Anarchy needed any help arriving at Hunter as a suspect. I glanced out the window. The man with the rumpled coat walked toward us. "Who's that?"

"Detective Peters, my new partner."

Since when had Anarchy had a partner? "Partner?"

Despite the afternoon sunshine shafting through the window and glinting off Anarchy's hair, the temperature in the room dropped by twenty-five degrees. "Partner."

*Ding dong.*

Marian didn't move. She was too engrossed with staring at the detective already in her house. I couldn't blame her. Caught in a ray of sunshine the way he was, Anarchy dazzled. He looked like a slightly cranky Greek god—if Greek gods wore plaid sport coats.

Aggie, who was completely unaffected by the sight of Anarchy in the sunlight, moved toward the door to the living room. "I'll get that." She jerked her sproingy red head toward the front hall. "If you don't mind, Mrs. Dixon."

"Mind?" Marian tore her gaze away from Anarchy. "Mind what?"

"Do you mind if I answer the door?"

"What door?"

*Ding dong.*

Apparently Anarchy's new partner was not a patient man.

Marian's hands fluttered near her neck. "The door. Yes, please answer the door. Thank you." Her gaze reverted to Anarchy.

Aggie rolled her eyes and disappeared into the living room.

"What can you tell me about the white Mercedes?" Anarchy shared a devastating smile with Marian. "Did you see a license plate?"

"No, I didn't." Marian shook her head as if disappointing Anarchy was the biggest regret of her life.

"Then why do you think the car was Tafft's?"

Marian managed to shift her gaze away from Anarchy to me. "His car is in the driveway so often. Who else could it belong to?"

Anarchy scowled.

"I spoke with Hunter after I called you. He was at his office. All the way downtown."

The scowl deepened.

"Definitely murder." Detective Peters spoke from the doorway. The man had to have smoked three packs a day for years to have that much gravel in his voice. Aggie stood behind him with her arms crossed over the blue of her muumuu. Something about the tilt of her head and the set of her mouth spoke of immediate dislike.

Peters, unaware that a woman who liked everyone had taken against him, continued, "Between the eyes. Small caliber bullet. I'd guess a .22."

Oh dear.

Anarchy closed his eyes and rubbed the bridge of his nose. "I don't suppose—" he opened his eyes "—you checked on your gun before you came over here?" He knew I was the owner of a .22.

"No. It should be in my nightstand." Please let the damned gun be in my nightstand.

Detective Peters dug a notepad out of his pocket, regarded me with beady eyes, and jotted something down. "You were the last person to see the victim?"

"Obviously not."

"There was someone else at the house?"

I nodded. "Whoever killed her."

Detective Peters' lips thinned. "Aside from the killer?"

"I suppose I was."

"What did you talk about?"

"Paneling. We discussed removing the paneling in the study. And the rug. Khaki was going to measure for a new rug."

"How well did you know the victim?" Peters patted his pockets as if he was searching for a pack of cigarettes.

"Not well."

"But you left her alone in your house?"

"I did."

"Do you make a habit of leaving strangers alone in your home?"

I glanced at Anarchy. He wore his cop face.

"No," I said. "I don't. But she wasn't a stranger. We knew scads of the same people." I was dating her ex-husband.

Detective Peters' beady-eyed stare made me feel like an insect pinned to a child's science board. "So you left Mrs. White alone and—"

"I went to pick up Aggie. Khaki wanted to take a few measurements, but Aggie needed me."

"How convenient for you."

Max, who'd been lounging at my feet, lifted his head and growled.

Peters turned his gaze on Aggie. "What time did Mrs. Russell pick you up?"

"Around twelve fifteen."

"And you came straight home?"

"Yes. We had groceries."

"Then what happened?"

"Mrs. White's car was in the driveway and the front door was ajar. We entered the house. Mrs. Russell called for Mrs. White and we took the groceries to the kitchen."

"The door was open?" Peters asked.

Why wasn't Anarchy proclaiming my innocence? He looked as cold and hard as the marble surrounding the fireplace in Marian's living room.

The chaise called to me. I sat. "The door was cracked not hanging open."

"Did you fail to close it when you left?"

"No."

"So you left a stranger in your home for twenty minutes and during that brief window of time—" Detective Peters held up two nearly touching fingers to demonstrate how brief a window twenty minutes was "—a second stranger gained access to your house, killed Mrs. White, and disappeared."

That was exactly right. But the way Detective Peters said it made the whole thing sound wildly improbable. He made it sound as if the simpler explanation—that I had killed Khaki then gone to pick up Aggie—was more likely.

"I already told you. Khaki wasn't a stranger. I just didn't know her well. As for the person who killed her, Khaki had to have opened the door for them. So maybe they weren't a stranger to her."

Aggie nodded. So did Max.

Detective Peters narrowed his beady eyes until they looked like raisins stuck in the day-old dough of his face. "Who do you think the second stranger was?" The sneer in his gravelly voice suggested he didn't believe in the stranger.

"Whoever drove the white Mercedes," said Marian.

We all looked out the window at my house and the driveway filled with Khaki's BMW, my Triumph, and a baker's dozen of police cars.

It was as that exact moment that Hunter Tafft arrived in his white Mercedes.

# THREE

When my daughter, Grace, was little, we invited every child in her class to her birthday parties. I particularly remembered the party the year she was in first grade. The children played party games like pin the tail on donkey and musical chairs and shrieked, swung a pole at a piñata groaning with candy and shrieked. Trip Michaels whacked someone in the head with the pole which caused even more shrieking. Then there was the jostling and shrieking to determine who got to sit next to the birthday girl when she opened her presents. Finally, the little darlings ate cake and ice cream—and shrieked some more. After two exhausting, soul-killing hours, the mothers arrived and took their sugar-filled progeny home. CeCe Lowell told me in advance that she'd be late. Laurie Michaels did not.

I took the children into the den, sat on the couch, and sipped an industrial-size glass of wine.

Grace sat on the floor and played with her new set of Easy Curl rollers, also known as giant tear-inducing snarls waiting to happen.

Bobby and Trip plonked themselves down a respectable distance from Grace and her girly curlers and engaged in a heated debate. If Superman and Batman fought each other, who would win?

"There's no way Batman would win in a fair fight." The stripes on Bobby's t-shirt were marked with chocolate syrup and his hair was mussed from a scuffle for a musical chair, but he managed an unexpected level of gravitas. "Superman has super powers."

Trip wrinkled his freckled nose. "Fair? Batman doesn't have

super powers. What he's got is a cool car and gadgets. It's fair if he uses them."

The argument grew heated. The boys' cheeks flushed and their eight-year-old hands tightened to fists.

"Boys." I offered up a smile that hardly had the energy to move my lips. "Does it matter?"

"Yes!" They agreed on something.

I sank farther into the couch and sipped my wine. Boys. They always had to know who ran the playground.

The granite line of Anarchy's jaw suggested men weren't much different.

Hunter climbed out of his cool car and glanced first at the hive of activity at my house then at Marian's home.

I snuck a peek at my watch. It had taken him just over twenty minutes to arrive. Damn.

I glanced at Aggie. Her brows were drawn. Her forehead was furrowed. She looked as worried as I felt. The alibi we'd constructed for Hunter lay in ruins at our feet. He could have killed Khaki then made it back to his office in time to answer the phone.

Marian tittered again. Apparently handsome men had that effect on her.

"Who is that?" Only Detective Peters didn't know Hunter.

Given the direction of Hunter's steps, that was about to change.

"The victim's ex-husband," said Anarchy.

"Ellison's boyfriend," said Marian.

Gah!

Aggie's lips curled slightly. Hunter was second to Bess in her affections, and now that Bess was gone...

I wasn't about to correct Marian; it would be like protesting too much.

Hunter, unaware that he was a newly minted murder suspect, strode toward us.

"I'll answer the door." Marian hurried out of the sunroom.

"So you and the victim's ex-husband are involved," said

Detective Peters. It was a statement not a question. One didn't need much imagination to see the wheels and cogs spinning above his head and reaching conclusions—wrong conclusions.

"Hunter and I are friends." I turned my gaze back to the street. So much better than looking at Detective Peters' smirk or the way Anarchy's jaw moved—almost as if he was grinding his teeth. I cleared my throat. "Um..."

"Will you look at that?" Aggie sounded positively peppy.

A second Mercedes, identical to Hunter's, parked next to the curb. A man climbed out of the car and stared at my house.

"Who is it?" she asked.

I took a deep breath, held it for five seconds, turned my head, and said in a calm voice that belied my inner cartwheels, "That is Stan White. Khaki's husband."

Detective Peters' nose twitched like a hunting dog's—one who'd just caught the scent of fresh prey.

Stan, unaware of the scrutiny of two homicide detectives, patted his comb-over, smoothed the lapels of his forest green and gold plaid jacket, and straightened his shoulders. Like Hunter, he looked first at my house then at Marian's. Unlike Hunter, he walked toward mine.

A uniformed police officer stopped him before he even stepped on the drive.

A lively conversation ensued. Stan talked with his hands, pointing at my house then turning his hands palms up in a plea.

The officer crossed his arms and shook his head.

"Good afternoon." Hunter spoke from the entrance to the sunroom. His jawline looked every bit as clenched as Anarchy's. Behind him, Marian wrung her hands. Were one handsome lawyer, one handsome detective, one surly detective, a neighbor, a housekeeper, and one dastardly dog more than she could handle?

"You're Hunter Tafft?" Detective Peters dragged his gaze away from Stan White's gesticulations. "Where were you between noon and one today?"

"I grabbed a sandwich and ate at my desk."

"Anyone who can corroborate that?"

"My secretary." Hunter glanced at Aggie. "And Mrs. DeLucci. I spoke with her on the phone."

Across the street, Stan waved his arms.

Detective Peters was missing an important point. How did Stan White know to come to my house?

If Anarchy's intense scowl was any indication, he hadn't missed that point.

"That was fast," said Marian. Murmured, really. I barely heard her.

"Fast?" I tilted my head to the side and shifted my gaze to my hostess.

"I called him—" she nodded toward Stan and his wind-milling arms "—when I got Detective Jones' coffee."

There was no doubt as to Mother's source on my comings and goings. "Did you tell him about Khaki?" My voice *might* have been a teensy bit chilly.

"Not exactly."

"What did you tell him?" A jeweler could have used Anarchy's tone to cut diamonds.

Marian crossed her hands over her chest. "That there was an incident." She glanced away from the people in the room. Her gaze settled on the owls hanging on her wall. Apparently their beaded eyes (as opposed to Detective Peters' beady eyes) bothered her. She shifted her gaze again. This time to the happenings in front of my house. "I told him he should get here quickly."

"He didn't ask what kind of incident?" asked Anarchy.

"No. He just said he'd come right away."

"So you didn't tell him his wife had been murdered?"

Marian's cheeks turned an unbecoming shade, somewhere between alizarin crimson and quinacridone magenta. "We didn't talk about his wife."

"He knew it was you calling?"

"Yes." The single word sounded like a teenage *of course* with a side of eye-roll.

"Then why is he trying to talk his way into Mrs. Russell's house rather than knocking on your door?"

"I'm sure I don't know."

"How well did you know Mrs. White?" The gravel in Detective Peters' voice sounded deeper, heavier, like river stones.

Marian blinked three times then shifted her attention to the rumpled detective. "Just socially. She's younger than I am, but we've sat on a few committees together over the years."

"You know her husband better?" asked Anarchy.

"Stan and I were grade school sweethearts."

Detective Peters rubbed his forehead. "What is the nature of your relationship now?"

Marian's hands flew to her throat. "You're not suggesting..."

"Just answer the question, ma'am."

"Eeeeh." It was the sound a helium balloon makes when you pull the stem tight and let the gas out slowly. Only it was coming from behind Marian's clenched teeth.

Max covered his ears with his paws. The rest of us looked at her with stunned expressions on our faces. Who knew a human could hit that note?

Then again, who knew a human could sustain such a sound for so long?

Max lifted his nose in the air and howled.

It was at that moment that Marian's cat padded into the sunroom. Perhaps it was curious about the strange sounds. If that was true, the old adage that curiosity killed the cat looked as if it might hold true.

Max lunged at Marian's prize-winning Persian.

I lunged for Max. "Bad dog!"

Of course I was too late—Max, with prey in his sights, was faster than a Lamborghini Countach.

The cat leapt into the air as if springs were attached to its paws.

What went up must come down.

And Max was waiting with the devil in his eyes.

*Yeowl.*

Leaping into thin air having failed as an escape route, the cat leapt for the wall and sank its claws into an unsuspecting macramé owl. The terrified animal climbed. Climbed then adhered. Like glue. When the cat lifted a paw, the owl lifted as well.

Max stood on his hind legs and rested his front paws against the wall.

"Max!" I sounded like Mother.

He ignored me. After all, the cat's bushy tail hung less than an inch from his grinning jaws.

*Yeowl.*

"Percival. Sweetheart." Baby talking her cat wasn't working. Percival was too smart for that. Marian planted her hands on her hips and glared at me. "Control your dog."

I was trying. "Max!"

Aggie clasped the leash onto Max's collar and hauled him off the wall.

Percival's tail twitched, but his hold on the owl remained resolute. Given the way his paws had pierced the owl's macramé heart, Percival probably didn't have much choice.

"I'll take him outside," said Aggie. She pulled on the leash, dragging a reluctant Max into the living room.

They appeared on the other side of the window. Aggie looked grim. Max looked as if he'd just had a grand adventure.

"Marian." I pressed my hands together as if I was praying for forgiveness. "I'm so sorry."

Like Max, Marian ignored me. Instead she directed her attention to the cat hanging on the wall. "Poor Percy-wercy. Did that big, nasty dog scare Mommy's baby?"

Hunter, Anarchy, and Detective Peters gaped at her.

Percival's enormous eyes tracked Max on the other side of the window.

"Come to Mommy." Marian held out her arms.

Percy lifted a paw and the owl lifted with him. *Yeowl.* Never before had I heard such an unhappy animal.

"He's stuck." Hunter stepped forward. "His claws are caught in the yarn. I'll get him down."

"No, I'll do it." Anarchy elbowed past him.

Percival scrabbled away from Anarchy's extended hands. *Hiss.*

Hunter reached for Percival.

*Hiss.* Louder this time, with more feeling.

Marian wrung her hands. "Percy, these nice men are trying to help you."

Percival didn't want their help.

"We have a murder to investigate." Detective Peters brushed past Anarchy and Hunter. He didn't reach for Percival. He reached for the owl. He pulled the macramé owl off the wall and the cat came with it, waving in the air like a fluffy, furious flag.

*Yeeeeeowl.* If Percival had been unhappy before...the sounds coming from him now pierced eardrums and expressed his extreme displeasure at the way his day was progressing.

The detective deposited the owl and the pussycat on the floor. Percival attacked the owl, clawing and biting his way free of the macramé trap. No one stepped forward to help. I, for one, did not want my hands shredded.

It was at that moment that Stan White appeared in the entrance to the sunroom and cleared his throat. "The woman with the dog let me in." When none of us reacted to this bit of news, he took a gunfighter stance—legs apart, hands hovering near his hips, a scowl darkening his face. "Where. Is. My. Wife?"

Percy especially paid him no mind. Instead he ripped through the few last stands of yarn and disentangled his traumatized self from the destroyed owl. Trailing bits of yarn and the twig that served as the owl's perch, the cat dashed through Stan's legs.

Again, Stan's arms rounded like a windmill. But now he tilted. Round and round and back.

Timber!

*Thunk.* He landed on his keister.

"Stan!" Marian rushed to his side. "Are you hurt?"

He smoothed his comb-over back into place (except for one

stray hank that stood straight up) and pushed himself onto his elbows. "I'm fine." He didn't sound fine. He sounded as mad as Marian's cat.

Detective Peters, Marian, and Stan glared at me as if Stan's misfortune was somehow *my* fault.

Anarchy's face was blank, distant—as if he was conjugating Latin verbs in his head.

Hunter's lips twitched and his eyes sparkled. The man was trying not to laugh.

None of them understood. Max wasn't a dog. He was a force of nature. One that couldn't be fully controlled by a mere human. Even now, outside on the lawn, he pulled on Aggie, no doubt eager to return to his pursuit of Percival.

"I should help Aggie with the dog." I moved toward the door.

"What are you going to do with him?" asked Detective Peters.

"Put him in the backyard."

"Eeeesh." The sharp inhalation of breath came from Marian.

"My backyard."

She exhaled.

"I'll help you." Anarchy stepped forward.

"It doesn't take three people to put a dog in a backyard." Detective Peters' eyes bulged slightly.

"You don't know that dog," Anarchy replied.

That ended the discussion.

Together we walked through Marian's living room and foyer and stepped out into the mild afternoon.

"You have a partner," I said.

"I do." The tone of his voice suggested he'd rather not talk about the rumpled detective in Marian's sunroom.

"Why?"

"All homicide detectives are assigned partners."

"You didn't have one before."

"Things change."

"And you really think you can work with that man?" That man suspected I'd killed a woman I barely knew. I didn't like being a murder suspect. Not. At. All. Of course, Anarchy once suspected I killed my husband, but that was somehow less offensive. There had existed a laundry list of good reasons for me to kill Henry. "He thinks I killed Khaki."

"He's just testing the waters." Mild. His tone had turned mild.

"He's testing the waters with Hunter and Marian and Stan too?" We reached Aggie and Max and I held out my hand for the leash.

"I've got him." Anarchy took Max's leash from Aggie.

"So everyone he meets is a potential suspect?"

"That about sums it up." He took a few steps across Marian's leaf-strewn yard, paused, and looked over his shoulder. "Watch what you say around him. You're his favorite."

# FOUR

When the police showed no signs of leaving, I asked Hunter to take Aggie home. They drove off in his white Mercedes. Out of sight probably didn't mean out of mind, but surely Detective Peters would realize that Khaki's current husband was a better suspect than her ex. At least I hoped he would.

If he came to that conclusion, he didn't share it with me.

At half past two, I called Grace's school and told them she needed to go to her grandparents' house after cheer practice.

At half past four, Detective Peters fixed his splenetic gaze on me. "We'll be here all night. You should find somewhere else to sleep."

I called the Alameda Hotel and booked a room. Of course, if Mother knew Grace and I were homeless for the night, she'd sigh and have guest rooms prepared for us. Mother hated last-minute plans. And unexpected houseguests definitely counted as last-minute plans. Any capital I earned by agreeing to buy a table at Cora's luncheon would be spent—and then some. Worse, I'd be unable to escape a lecture on the perils of finding bodies. Despite Mother's belief to the contrary, I was already familiar with the perils of finding bodies. She had nothing new to add.

I climbed into my car, drove to Mother and Daddy's, and pulled into the drive. Grace pulled in behind me. Perfect timing for once.

"What's up?" she asked.

I didn't see any gentle way to tell her. "Khaki White was murdered in your father's study."

"Who?"

"She was a decorator."

"That's awful. Are you okay?"

"I am."

She pushed a few strands that had escaped from her ponytail away from her face and regarded her grandparents' home with a slight frown on her face. "Why are we here?"

"The police are still at our house. Unfortunately, it doesn't look like they'll finish anytime soon. I booked us a room at the Alameda."

Grace cut her gaze toward Mother's house. "Does Granna know?"

"About the murder? Yes."

She shook her head. Her granna's omniscience when it came to things in my life going sideways was unquestioned. "No. Does she know that we're staying in a hotel?"

"If we stay at the Alameda, we won't disrupt her household. You leave for school so early, and—" I searched for another reason "—if your grandparents have plans, I'd hate to have them cancel on our account." And there was that inevitable lecture I wanted to avoid.

"Are we going in?"

We were parked in the drive. Conversing in the drive. We could hardly avoid saying *hello*.

We marched up the front walk. I *might* have looked a bit grim, because Grace reached out and squeezed my hand. I smoothed my expression, less Marie Antoinette on her way to the guillotine, more Marie Antoinette on her way to eat cake.

Mother's housekeeper, Penelope, opened the front door. "I'm sorry, Mrs. Russell, your parents are out for the evening."

"Really?" I sounded too perky. "At this hour?" It wasn't quite five o'clock.

She nodded. "They're having dinner with Mr. and Mrs. Knight. Mrs. Walford went early to go over plans for a luncheon."

Of course she had. Mother was probably explaining everything

Cora needed to do to make the event a success. Resign and put Mother in charge.

If Thornton was there, he was probably wondering aloud why Cora hadn't asked Mother for help from the start.

If Daddy was there, he was probably drinking a dry martini and wishing he was home watching Walter Cronkite on the evening news.

"I didn't realize they had plans this evening. Please tell them we stopped by."

Grace and I retraced our steps to our cars.

"Meet me at the Alameda?"

"I don't have anything to wear to school tomorrow."

"Meet me at Swanson's?"

That earned a smile.

I parked in Swanson's garage and counted three white Mercedes in the lot. Funny how one didn't notice things like the color of cars until murder made them important.

Grace and I shopped until the stores closed. Shopped enough that the police could take a week to complete their tasks at the house and Grace wouldn't have to repeat outfits. Neither would I.

We drove the few blocks to the hotel, parked (another three white Mercedes), and carried our bags to the room. Hanging up the new clothes took only a few minutes (so many of them were still on hangers). Fresh lipstick and a much needed comb later, we rode the elevator to the lobby and were seated in the Pam-Pam Room with a view of the Plaza.

"What happened?"

"I ran up to Milgrim's to pick up Aggie. When we got back, Khaki was dead." I took a sip of water. Where was the waiter? I wanted a drink. "Khaki was shot."

"People have died at the house before and we haven't had to leave."

True. But things had changed. "Anarchy has a new partner."

"He does? What's he like?"

"He's short and rumpled and he suspects I killed Khaki."

"That's ridiculous. Why didn't Detective Jones set him straight?"

An excellent question. Where was the waiter? I craned my neck.

"Who do you think killed her?"

"No idea."

"Why our house?"

I shook my head. "I don't know."

"Do you think we'll be able to go home tomorrow?"

"I hope so."

"It's creepy to think she died in our house." Grace shuddered. "I mean inside."

There'd been more than one body found outside the house. Khaki was the first to die within its walls. "You're right. It is creepy. We can stay here longer if you feel uncomfortable going home."

"I'd just like to know *why*. You don't think someone was trying to kill you?"

"No."

A furrow appeared between Grace's brows. "You're sure?"

"I'm sure."

"I'd still like to know why."

That made two of us.

"What are your plans for tomorrow?" Grace asked.

"They're in flux."

"Would you stop by the club, pick up my tennis racket, and bring it to school?"

"Is it in your locker?"

"No. I had it restrung. It's in the pro-shop."

"Sure," I said.

"I need it by the end of the day. Trip and I are meeting for tennis after school."

"Trip?"

"Trip Michaels."

If the kid hit a tennis ball as hard as he hit a piñata, Grace was in for a game.

*  *  *

I waited at the counter and ignored a saucy wink from a tennis dress I did not need. The dress winked again. It even upped the ante with a come-hither smile.

No.

I did not need another tennis dress. Did. Not. Looking at the price tag never hurt anyone. I reached for the tag—

"Ellison!" Jane Addison stood in front of me in a white tennis dress with a navy blue sweater draped around her shoulders. Jane was to gossip what martinis were to gin. She had an acquisitive gleam in her eye, and I resigned myself to an interrogation.

The tennis dress pouted. Its flirtation had been going so well.

"What are you doing here?" Jane demanded.

"Picking up a racket for Grace." And almost resisting the lure of another tennis dress.

"But I heard..."

Of course everyone knew that Khaki had been found shot at my house. Marian Dixon had probably spent all of last night spreading the word.

Jane glanced around the shop, spotted the pro emerging from the back room with Grace's racket, and lowered her voice. "It was definitely murder? I mean she didn't trip and hit her head or fall down the stairs or—"

"Definitely murder. I didn't realize you knew Khaki."

"Not well. Of course, I'd heard a few things—"

"Oh?" On occasion, it was quite handy to know the biggest gossip in town. Maybe Jane knew why someone had shot Khaki.

"It wouldn't be right to speak ill of the dead."

She was playing coy? Now? There was no midwestern equivalent for the southern *bless her heart*, the phrase most often used when southern ladies pulled out their knives. If there was an equivalent, Jane would use it every day. Five times a day every day. And after she'd uttered that equivalent, she'd speak ill of the dead, the cheating, the divorcing, the dieting, the sick, the engaged, and the widowed. Jane seldom played coy. Whatever she knew about Khaki had to be salacious. She was building suspense.

"You're right."

I refused to play her game.

Her forehead puckered and her gaze fell to the floor. She'd hoped for a breathless *you can tell me*, and I'd disappointed her. If she didn't offer up some juicy item, she could hardly ask me insider details about Khaki's murder. I closed my eyes and imagined the infuriated expression on Detective Peters' truculent face if he learned I'd shared details of his investigation. Much as I wanted to hear what Jane knew, the wise path was to avoid gossip.

Jane opened her mouth and closed it. A goldfish out of water and gasping for air. Well, if one replaced *air* with gossip.

The door to the pro-shop swung open and Linda Connor stepped inside. "Jane, we're waiting. Are you coming?" She noticed me and added, "Good morning, Ellison."

"Good morning."

Jane and Linda were the unlikeliest of doubles partners. Linda shot straight, didn't gossip, and cared more about being on time than the latest news.

"Coming," said Jane. "I'm coming." She looked at me and her eyes narrowed. "Jinx is taking a lesson on the back court. You should say hello to her before you leave." With that she walked through the door Linda held open for her.

Jinx was part of my regular bridge foursome. That Jane thought I should see her tennis lesson was worrisome. I tightened my grip on Grace's racket. "Thank you." I held up the racket and waved it at the pro behind the counter. Molly! That was the young woman's name. "Molly, with whom is Mrs. George taking a lesson?"

"Clint." Neither her face nor her tone revealed an ounce of emotion. They were carefully blank. Oh, dear. What was Jinx up to on the back court?

I stepped outside. Despite the mild weather, most of the courts were empty. Women tended to schedule around what they thought the weather would be, and November meant cold and blustery.

That meant bridge in a cozy card room or a book club meeting in a living room warmed by a fire. It did not mean tennis lessons.

I could have ignored Jane's broad hint or Molly's lack of inflection, but together—well, I had to know. I meandered toward the back court.

Jinx stood on the baseline with her hands wrapped around the handle of a racket. Clint stood behind her with his arms wrapped around her. His hands covered hers. Together they practiced a backhand swing.

Innocent enough, except that they stood far too close, her backside snuggled up against his tennis shorts.

Jinx had modern ideas. She'd sold several generations' worth of antiques for a sleeker look. Gone was the Chippendale dining room set her grandmother had cherished. In came a white Eero Saarinen table and tulip chairs. But this—this snuggling—was proof that her modern ideas extended to marriage. Did Preston know?

I shifted my gaze somewhere safer—the carefully painted lines on the court. The lines that told players if a ball was inbounds. Or, as seemed to be the case, very much out of bounds.

Ugh.

Jinx spotted me and pulled away from Clint's embrace.

Perhaps not the best idea. Compelling evidence existed that Clint had enjoyed the rub of Jinx's tennis skirt against his shorts.

Double ugh.

I shifted my gaze to their feet. Jinx wore Tretorns and socks with little white pom-poms at the back of her ankles. Someone once told me the pom-poms kept the socks from slipping. If that was true, Jinx needed much bigger pom-poms. What I saw represented major slippage.

Jinx crossed the court, the expression on her face sheepish. She'd been caught. With a tennis pro. She was a walking cliché.

I nodded in Clint's direction. "I credited you with more imagination."

"There's nothing wrong with Clint."

I studied the man on the court. He wore short white shorts

(thankfully the tent had subsided), a white shirt that clung too closely to his chest muscles, tube socks with blue stripes, and Adidas tennis shoes. A furrow marred the still-tanned expanse of his forehead until he caught me looking. Then he manufactured a grin—all white teeth and doubtful sincerity. To the casual observer, he looked as if he might lose an intelligence battle with an orangutan.

My face must have reflected my thoughts, because Jinx glanced his way. "I know. I know. But he's pretty to look at and—" a satisfied smile spread across her face "—he's got a serve and volley you wouldn't believe."

*La la la la.* I refrained from covering my ears. Barely. "Have you lost your mind?"

"If Preston gets a mid-life crisis, I deserve one too."

It takes two. Two to fall in love. Two to get married. Two to rip a marriage to shreds. "Preston?" Cheating? I couldn't reconcile the Preston George I knew—middle-aged waistline, thick glasses, kind smile—with a cheater. "With whom?"

"You wouldn't believe me if I told you."

"Try me." A certain dryness may have colored my tone.

"Khaki White."

I blinked. "Khaki White, the decorator?"

"Do you know another Khaki White?"

I couldn't wrap my head around the idea. Preston and Khaki? I didn't see it. "Khaki White who was murdered at my house yesterday?"

Jinx dropped her racket. The wooden frame clattered against the court's hard surface. "*What?*" Her face was slack, as if I'd just delivered shocking news.

"I'm sorry. I assumed everyone between St. Louis and Denver had heard."

"No. I—" she rubbed the bridge of her nose with the heel of her palm "—I was busy yesterday. I let the machine get the phone." Jinx lowered her hand and stared at me with worried eyes. "Murdered. You're sure?"

"Positive."

"When was she killed?"

"Around lunchtime yesterday."

"Do the police know who did it?"

"I don't think so. Last I checked, I was a suspect."

She waved my being a suspect aside with a bend of her wrist that did not bode well for her backhand. "Your detective knows better."

Maybe Anarchy knew better. Detective Peters remained unconvinced.

"Lunchtime? You're sure?" She looked ten years older than when I'd arrived on the court three minutes ago.

"Between noon and twelve thirty."

Jinx crouched and picked up her fallen racket. "I have to go. I'll call you."

Without so much as a glance at Clint of the memorable serve and volley, she walked off the court. Trotted off the court. As if she had a burning question that needed answering.

"Jinx," I called after her.

She paused.

"Jane Addison sent me back here."

That the biggest gossip in town knew Jinx had been carrying on with a tennis pro should have been cause for concern. Major concern.

Jinx's racket bounced against the side of her leg. Once. Twice. Three times. "It doesn't matter now." She resumed her trot, leaving me alone with Clint.

What was so important that she could so easily set aside the damage sure to be caused by Jane's loose talk?

I glanced at Clint. He looked crestfallen at Jinx's sudden departure. The man had to be in his late twenties. Surely he'd figured out by now that there were more important things in life than a great serve and volley.

"I don't think she's coming back," I said.

He peered at this watch.

"She paid for an hour and it's only a quarter after. Do you want the rest of her lesson?"

Definitely not. I had better things to think about—like why Jinx suspected her husband of Khaki's murder.

# FIVE

Clouds heavy with rain chased away the morning sun and the temperature dropped by at least thirty degrees in fifteen minutes. I should have seen this change coming—would have seen this change coming if I weren't avoiding the television. But who wants to see their home identified as a murder scene on the morning news?

The fleet of squad cars decorating my drive had been reduced to one. Some kind soul had even removed Khaki's BMW. A yellow taxi cab idled in its place. Aggie stood next to the driver's window. She wore a pom-pom-fringed poncho in shades of avocado green and harvest gold over a pumpkin-hued muumuu, and she glared into the bottom of her worn leather purse—the enormous one painted with cheerful daisies. Perhaps she glared because the bag seemed to have swallowed her whole arm.

I pulled in behind them.

Aggie abandoned the waiting driver and marched up to my car. "Do you have two dollars?"

"Of course." I pulled my billfold out of my much smaller purse (no daisies—not judging—well, not much), withdrew a five, and handed it to her.

She accepted the bill, stalked back to the driver, shoved the five through the open window, and waited while he counted her change. With a scowl that would have sent me running for the hills, she gave him a single back.

The man screeched down the drive.

Max, whose tail wagged with gratitude for being picked up

from the doggie boarding house, and I got out of the car and approached her. Slowly. Carefully. Aggie in a bad mood was something new. "Rough morning?"

"I'm not good at the bus. I got on what I thought was the right number and ended up miles from here." She handed me two dollars. "I have to buy a car."

I stuffed the money in my pocket. "I've been thinking about that. You do so much driving for Grace and me. Why don't I buy a car for you to drive?"

"Don't be ridiculous."

A gust of wind on a fast track from Canada barreled into us. I shivered and wished for a hat—a new one, felt with a floppy brim. "I'm not being ridiculous. Lots of people drive company cars. Let's go in before we freeze."

We almost made it. Almost.

"You've disrupted the neighborhood again." Margaret Hamilton was a certified witch (well, not *really* certified. They didn't have tests for that sort of thing. But, if they did, she'd earn a perfect score). She was also my next-door neighbor. Today, like most days, she wore black. Black pointy shoes. Black coat. Black muffler wrapped around her scrawny neck. Black and an evil scowl on her pinched face.

Max growled. Thank God I'd put a leash on him. I tightened my hold. "I assure you, I did not kill Khaki White."

"You and that dog are nothing but trouble."

Max growled again. Deeper this time.

"I'm sorry if the police disturbed you, but it was hardly my fault." I didn't complain when she donned her witch outfit and rode her broomstick. She shouldn't complain when a body showed up at my house.

"I want the police out of here."

In that, we were in agreement. "They're almost done." Surely the reduction in police cars meant they'd nearly finished processing the crime scene.

Margaret sniffed and turned on her heel.

Aggie, who'd remained silent, muttered, "I'll get you, my pretty, and your little dog too."

I laughed. I couldn't help it.

Margaret spun and glared at me.

Perfect. Now she'd hex me. Again. "Aggie was just saying we made it four whole days without incident."

Now Margaret's glare included Aggie.

"I'm sure things will calm down." I wasn't sure of that. Not at all. "I apologize for any inconvenience."

Margaret sniffed again.

Neither Aggie nor I said a word until she was off the property. Even Max refrained from growling.

I opened the front door and we stepped inside.

A uniformed policeman with a cup of coffee in his right hand sat on the steps to the second floor. A bag from a nearby donut shop sat to his left. Powdered sugar dusted his mustache.

He stood and the powdered sugar that had missed his mustache and landed in his lap fell like snow.

"Good morning, officer. I'm Ellison Russell."

Max pulled on his leash, his gaze fixed on the bag of donuts.

"Officer Smith."

"Are you almost done?"

Officer Smith's glance shifted between the bag of donuts and my hungry dog.

"In the study," I added.

A dull red darkened his cheeks. "Yes, ma'am."

"Wonderful. If you'll grab your breakfast, I'll let Max off his leash. May we look?" I jerked my chin toward the study.

"Of course."

Aggie and I crossed the foyer and peered into the room where Khaki died. My heart sank and Aggie's sharp intake of breath told me all I needed to know about her opinion. I looked at her anyway.

Aggie regarded the study, now covered with fingerprint dust, with a look usually reserved for...Well, Mother wore that exact look the night Kitty Ballew got drunk at the club's summer cocktail party, disappeared for twenty minutes, and reappeared with her dress on inside out. It was a look of total and utter disapproval.

"Coffee," I said. "We need coffee before we can even think about this mess." Mr. Coffee might not be able to solve all the world's problems or clean the study, but things tended to look brighter after he'd worked his magic.

I headed for the kitchen.

Mr. Coffee waved *hello*. His bright yellow gingham face never failed to bring a smile to mine. This morning was no exception.

Aggie tsked. Yesterday's groceries still sat on the counter. "I did put the perishables away." She pulled a box of Life cereal out of a bag and carried it to the pantry.

I took Mr. Coffee's pot, filled it with water, then filled his reservoir. Next I placed a filter in his basket-thingy and scooped coffee. Aggie needed some of his magic. And quickly.

The light on the answering machine blinked. Lord only knew the number of messages it held.

I glanced at Mr. Coffee. *Go ahead*, he said. *I'll have coffee ready for you soon.*

I pushed the button.

"Ellison?" A voice quavered. "This is Karen Fleming calling." Then came a pause as if she expected the answering machine to say, *how lovely to hear from you*. That was just silly. Mr. Coffee was the only talking appliance at my house. "I need to speak with you," Karen continued. "If I don't hear from you, I'll be there at ten tomorrow morning."

I glanced at my watch. The time read five minutes to ten. And tomorrow was today. Dammit.

What could Karen Fleming possibly want? And why? I barely knew the woman. She was older, didn't play much bridge, and had earned herself a reputation as an unreliable committee member. Good when she showed up—if she showed up—but not someone a woman could trust with an important job. All that meant I seldom saw her.

*Ding dong.*

I sighed. "I'll get that."

My feet may have dragged on the way to the front door. I definitely paused and took a deep breath before I turned the handle and pulled it open.

My best friend Libba stood on the other side. "I've been trying to reach you all night. What the hell happened?"

I stood aside and she pushed into the foyer, a miffed whirlwind dressed in jeans, to-die-for boots, a ruana, and a felt hat with a floppy brim.

I closed the door behind her. "Where did you find your hat?"

She adjusted the brim. "Swanson's. What happened over here yesterday?"

"Swanson's? I was there last night, and I didn't see a hat like that."

"That's because I'd already bought it. Now, what happened?"

Officer Donut appeared in the foyer. A second officer followed. "We're done here, Mrs. Russell. Detective Peters asks that you stay out of the study."

"For how long?"

"Until you hear differently."

That meant a reprieve from cleaning. I didn't argue. "Fine. Thank you, officers."

With curious glances at Libba, they exited the front door.

"What. Happened?" Libba crossed her arms and positively glared at me.

"Someone murdered Khaki White."

"I already know that." Frustration raised her pitch. "And?"

"I came home from grocery shopping and found her dead in the study."

"That's it?" Libba twisted her mouth, seemingly unconvinced.

"That's it. Now I have a question for you."

"What?"

"Is Jinx's husband—" Damn. "—*was* Preston George having an affair with Khaki?"

"She told you that?"

"She did." I refrained from mentioning Jinx's own dalliances. Besides, chances were that Libba already knew all about Clint's serve and volley. Probably first hand.

Libba adjusted the brim of her hat. "Preston and Khaki were on the board of some charity together. Something to do with poor women with bad husbands. But the two of them? Together? I just don't see it. What I want to know is—"

"The coffee is ready," Aggie called from outside the kitchen door.

"Come on." I jerked my head toward the kitchen.

Libba answered with a put-upon sigh.

Steaming mugs waited for us on the kitchen island. I wrapped my hands around one, enjoying the warmth that seeped through the porcelain. "Thank you, Aggie."

"You're welcome." She pulled a box of Super Sugar Crisp from the last remaining grocery bag. Super Sugar Crisp? Grace and I were going to have to chat about the foods she added to Aggie's grocery list.

Libba picked up the second mug. "Thanks."

Aggie, whose mood had not sweetened at all, grumbled.

*Ding dong.*

"That must be Karen Fleming," I said.

"Karen Fleming? What's she doing here?" Libba was in a mood similar to Aggie's. Sour. Grumpy. Cross. Although, to the best of my knowledge, Libba's car hadn't died, nor had she helped find a body, or been interrogated by the police. Aggie deserved my sympathies. Libba did not.

"I haven't the slightest."

Libba followed me to the front door. She grumbled the whole way.

I opened the door. Karen stood on the other side.

"Karen." I manufactured a smile. "Welcome."

She ventured inside. "Good morning."

Was her nose red from the cold or had she been crying?

"It's very nice of you to see me." She stared at Libba's boots.

"Nice to see you too, Libba."

Libba pasted something on her face that was probably supposed to be a smile but looked more like a grimace. Libba *cared* about clothes and hair and the way one presented oneself to the world. Karen wasn't more than ten years older than us, but she looked as if she was one of Mother's contemporaries. The clothes didn't help her. At all. A house dress in a zig-zag pattern that tried to look like Missoni and failed worn under a shapeless wool coat. Sensible shoes. And her hair—a bouffant a la 1962.

Karen's lips thinned as if she understood all the disapproval in Libba's expression. A single tear ran down her cheek.

I rubbed my forehead. I was a terrible hostess. The poor woman was in distress, and I was running a mental inventory of her ensemble. I was as bad as Libba. "Are you all right? Let's go sit in the living room. I'll have Aggie bring you some coffee."

Actually, I'd get the coffee. Aggie deserved a day of mourning for Bess without my bothering her for little things.

"Have a seat." I led Karen to the living room and waved at the seating arrangement nearest the fireplace. "How do you take your coffee?"

"Cream and sugar." Another tear. "Actually, black. I ran into Daniel the other day and he said I'd gained a few pounds."

Daniel Fleming needed to have his eyesight tested. Karen was the kind of thin most women dreamed of. "Nonsense. And besides, who cares what he thinks? You're not married to him anymore. I'll be back in a jiff."

When I returned, Karen was seated on the couch with her ankles crossed and her hands neatly folded in her lap. Libba, whose spine could contort into odd shapes, lounged in a wingback. They weren't talking.

I set the tray on the coffee table, poured a cup for Karen, topped off Libba's near-empty mug, reclaimed my own coffee, and chose the wingback that matched Libba's. Unlike Libba, I actually sat.

Karen took a sip of her coffee. "I came about Khaki."

Libba shifted in her chair.

"Oh?" My rate of coffee consumption wasn't high enough to craft a clever reply.

"She was a good decorator." Karen daubed at her eyes with a handkerchief. "A good friend."

Khaki, in her stacked boots and short skirt, and the frumpy woman on the couch had been good friends? "Oh?" Lack of coffee or not, I needed to step up my game. "I didn't realize you knew each other."

Karen nodded. Emphatically. "We hired her to redo the downstairs." She glanced down at her lap. "Daniel says I'm hopeless at that sort of thing. At any rate—" she looked up and her expression dared us to argue "—Khaki and I met and became friends."

"I'm so sorry for your loss." It sounded better than *oh.*

Karen covered her mouth with her free hand and a new wave of tears wet her cheeks.

I should have stuck with *oh.*

Libba shot me a look—one that said *what have you gotten us into?*

I didn't know Karen well. Perhaps she was given to big emotions. Even so, her response to Khaki's death seemed outsized. Or maybe not. Maybe a murder required a big response. Maybe my own response—mild regret with a side of concern—wasn't enough. After all, a woman was dead. I should be mourning her loss, not thinking about removing fingerprint dust from the study or if the fabric designer responsible for Karen's dress really meant to use that burnt umber shade.

"Khaki's death was a terrible tragedy," I said.

Karen nodded but said nothing, apparently waiting for more from me. That, or she was too overcome to speak.

"A terrible crime," I added.

She remained mute.

"A terrible loss."

"If you only knew." Her voice cracked and she fell silent.

Libba sat up. "What don't we know?"

Karen went quiet again. She shook her head sadly rather than answer the question.

Two—or three—could play mute. I inspected my cuticles. Ragged as usual. Wiping your hands with turpentine or mineral spirits would do that.

The silence stretched.

Karen broke first. "You found her?"

"I did."

"Did she suffer? Did her attacker hurt her?"

Khaki's attacker put a bullet in her brain. "I think it was quick. Why do you ask?"

"No reason." The words came too quickly. Karen might not have been scratching her nose (my own tell), but she was definitely lying.

I studied the woman on the couch. She looked as if the wrong words might shatter her. I swallowed the obvious question.

Libba, God love her, did not. "Do you know who killed her?"

"No. Of course not. No." Karen recoiled, plastering her spine against the back of the sofa, a physical retreat from the question.

She did know. Or she thought she did. "You're sure? "I know the investigating detective. I can call him if you'd like to talk."

"I shouldn't have come." Karen stood, bumping her knee against the corner of the coffee table hard enough to rattle the china. It was the sort of minor injury that hurt like hell. She seemed not to notice. "I have to go."

She snatched her purse off the couch and dashed toward the foyer.

I rose and followed her, catching her by the front door where she was having difficulties with the lock.

"I'll do that."

She lowered her head and stepped aside. "I'm so sorry to have bothered you."

I jiggled the lock just right and opened the door. "Karen, if you're in trouble, I know people who can help. I can help."

"I'm not in trouble." She lifted her gaze from the carpet. Something desperate and angry and sad burned in her eyes. "I can't believe you think I am."

She slipped outside, hurried to her car, and sped away—all without looking back.

Libba joined me in the foyer. "Do you think she knows who killed Khaki?"

I rubbed my suddenly tense neck. "No. I think she's worried she'll be next."

# SIX

I rested my head against the solid oak of the front door. Why did I have to be the one to find bodies, discover murders, and deal with unbridled emotions? Surely there were other women much better suited to drama? Libba, for instance.

Behind us someone cleared her throat.

I lifted my head and turned.

"Mrs. Walford is on the phone," said Aggie.

Again, why me? Usually Aggie put Mother off. "Tell her I'm—"

"She's very insistent." Maybe Aggie didn't feel up to creating smoke screens today. Lord knew I didn't feel up to a conversation with Mother.

"I'll take it in the stu—" Per Officer Donut, the study was off limits. "I'll take it in the family room." I turned to Libba. "Excuse me, please."

I hurried into the living room and grabbed my coffee cup (a morning chat with Mother required coffee).

Libba followed me, sank onto the couch, dug in her oversize purse, pulled out a copy of *Vogue*, and waved me away. "I'll wait."

Joy.

In the family room, Max lifted his head off the arm rest of the couch. His perfect morning included a visit outside where he took care of doggy business and completed a quick squirrel patrol. Next came a biscuit and a long nap.

I'd disturbed the nap part. "Sorry."

He grunted.

I steeled myself and picked up the receiver. "Hello."

"I hope you don't keep everyone waiting on the phone like this." Mother's version of hello when she was in a *mood.*

"Karen Fleming stopped by. I was seeing her out."

"Karen Fleming? What was she doing there?"

"No idea." It was God's truth.

"I want you to bring a check by the house this afternoon. Around four thirty or five."

"A check?"

Mother's deep sigh was perfectly crafted to communicate disappointment and evoke guilt. "Don't tell me you've forgotten already. You promised you'd sponsor a table at Cora's luncheon."

I had forgotten, safe in the knowledge that she'd never let me forget. "I'll drop it in the morning mail."

"No. Come by. Cora will be here. Thornton, too." She said her cousin's name as if seeing him was an incentive. Thornton was the closest thing Mother had to a brother and she adored him, which worked out well because Thornton adored being adored.

"Fine." Agreeing was easier than arguing. I wouldn't stay.

"Have they caught the killer yet?" she asked.

"Not that I know of."

Another sigh. This one annoyed. I could imagine her on the other end of the line—brows lowered, mouth a tight line. If she didn't have the receiver in her hand, she'd cross her arms. "Did you see the news?"

"No. I avoided watching."

"That neighbor of yours was interviewed."

"Which one?"

"Margaret Hamilton. She talked about you as if you were the Zodiac Killer. I want you to call Hunter and file a libel suit."

"What did she say?"

"That Khaki White was the third murder victim found at your house this year."

Unfortunately, that wasn't libelous. That was true. "It's not as if I killed any of them."

"That doesn't matter. People say where there's smoke, there's fire. I've told you, this has to stop."

"Mother, it's not as if I'm doing anything to make this happen. Believe me, if I were, I'd stop."

She tsked.

"I do not go looking for trouble. It finds me."

"I suppose that police detective is hanging around again." She made Anarchy sound as welcome as a disease—a really bad one like leprosy or syphilis.

"I haven't seen him today. Listen, Mother. Libba is here. I'll see you this afternoon. Bye." I hung up before she could argue.

What I'd told her was God's truth. I didn't look for trouble. This time Hunter was responsible for sending trouble my way.

I reclaimed the receiver and dialed.

Now Max sighed. Deeply.

The same cool, professional voice as yesterday answered the phone. "Law office."

"May I please speak with Mr. Tafft?"

"Who may I say is calling?"

"Ellison Russell."

"One moment, please."

I stared out the window where the wind spun a few unraked leaves in circles.

"Ellison." Hunter's voice was warm and welcoming as a cozy fire on a cold November morning.

"Hunter, I have a question."

"Shoot."

I cringed. There'd been entirely too much shooting of late. "Um, why did you ask me to call Khaki about redoing the study?"

"She asked me to."

"Pardon?"

"I told her you'd fired your last decorator. Khaki asked me to recommend her."

My spine stiffened. My neck stiffened. My scalp stiffened. "You discussed me with your ex-wife?"

"No." Hunter's voice was soothing, calming, as if he could sense my annoyance through the phone line. "We discussed the murder. That you'd fired your decorator came up in the course of the conversation."

Reasonable enough, but still unsettling. "Why did she want the job? Having her here was a bit—" I searched for the right word "—awkward."

"I wondered that too. I even asked her if working for you might be uncomfortable."

"What did she say?"

"She said that there were more important things at stake."

"What? What important things?"

"She had one of those national decorating magazines interested in doing an article. She was looking for the right project."

*A Masculine Study becomes a Feminine Retreat.* The headline scrolled across my brain. The only problem with that story was that national magazines like *Architectural Digest* and *House Beautiful* usually did articles on whole houses not individual rooms. Khaki had lied to Hunter. "Did she need the money?"

"No."

Maybe Hunter was wrong. Maybe Khaki needed the job and hadn't wanted to tell him. Lord knew we hadn't talked about important things. "She didn't come in with big ideas. All we talked about was which shade to stain the paneling."

"I don't know what to tell you, Ellison. Khaki thought she could get national exposure if she worked for you."

Which was patently ridiculous. "Why didn't you tell me this before?"

"You mean yesterday when Jones' new partner looked ready to arrest us both?"

"No. I mean before I called her."

On the couch, Max opened one eye. This conversation was taking entirely too long for his doggy tastes.

"I should have. I meant to. I'm sorry." Hunter and contrition. Two words that did not go together. Yet he sounded genuinely sorry. "I had a brief due, and I figured you were more than capable of handling anything Khaki came up with."

That was somewhat flattering. Too bad Khaki had somehow come up with murder.

"Let me make it up to you," he continued. "Let me take you to dinner tonight."

Grace was spending the evening with her friend, Donna. If I went, Aggie could skip making dinner. Given her current mood, taking a chore off her to-do list was appealing.

"I'll take you to Nabil's." One of my favorites.

"Um..."

"Just say yes, Ellison. Give Aggie the night off."

"Okay." It was a less than exuberant acceptance.

"I'll pick you up at six."

"See you then. Goodbye." I hung up the phone.

"I thought you were done with men." Libba spoke from the doorway.

"I am."

"You are? Because I believe I just heard you accept a date. The only question, was it with Hunter or Detective Jones?" She rubbed her chin. "Given that your detective is investigating a murder, I'm betting Hunter."

"He's not *my* detective, and you should mind your own business." Wasted breath on my part. After a lifetime of sticking her nose in my affairs, why would she stop now?

"Fine. Let's talk Khaki White."

"Why?"

Libba blinked. "What do you mean why?"

"Why do you want to talk about Khaki? I am sick—" I edited out *to death* "—of talking about dead people."

"This is hard on you, isn't it?" Libba actually looked sympathetic.

"What do you think?" Oh dear Lord. I sounded pathetic.

"I think if I couldn't make it through a week without finding a corpse, I'd be cranky too."

"I'm not cranky."

"Of course you're not." Her voice was pitched to frazzled-mother-negotiating-with-a-fractious-toddler.

"I'm not!" Maybe I was. A little.

"Go upstairs. Take a hot bath. Relax. We can talk later." She held up her hands and backed down the hallway toward the kitchen.

Soothing hot water. Scented bubbles. A divine prospect. But I knew something that would make me feel even better. "Aggie," I called. "Grab your poncho. I'm going to buy you a car."


A plumber's truck was parked in Mother and Daddy's driveway, so I parked at the curb. Their street, which was usually as busy as the club on a Monday night (that is to say, empty), was full of cars. A black Jaguar, a red VW Beetle similar to the one I'd just bought Aggie, a blue Cadillac, even a white Mercedes. Another one? I'd never noticed how many white Mercedes there were until one loomed large in my life. Then again, I probably hadn't notice red Bugs until today either.

I shook off my consideration of cars, glanced at my watch, marched up the front walk with my checkbook at the ready, and rang the bell.

Cora answered Mother's door. That was new. Mother's housekeeper usually answered the door, not one of her guests.

"Ellison, how lovely to see you. Come in." Cora stepped back, making room for me to enter. "May I take your coat?"

"I can't stay."

"Of course you can." Mother spoke from the entrance to the living room.

"No, I can't. I'm going out to dinner with Hunter." If ever there was news designed to keep Mother off my back, that was it.

As expected, she smiled brightly. For a half-second. "You're wearing that?"

There was nothing wrong with the navy slacks and white

turtleneck I wore beneath my trench coat. Not one thing. There was also no upside in pointing that out. "I need some time to get ready."

Thornton appeared behind Mother. He rested his hand on her shoulder. "I think she looks lovely, Frances. Very chic."

"Don't be silly, Thornton. What do you know about women's clothes?"

A shadow crossed over Thornton's face. "Hear that, Ellison? I've been put in my place. Listen to your mother."

"I always do." A statement so ridiculous no one bothered refuting it. "I brought my checkbook. How much should I write the check for?"

"A million dollars," said Thornton.

Mother laughed. Cora and I did not.

"That's a bit rich for my blood. What's the top sponsor level?"

"Twenty-five hundred," Cora replied.

"Done." I reached into my purse for a pen.

"I'm going to host a benefactors' party here at the house," said Mother. "You'll come?" It wasn't a question.

"I have an opening to get ready for."

"I'm sure you can make time for family."

The Clint Eastwood look—the narrow-eyed squint that said he'd love to shoot someone. I needed *that* look. I didn't have that look. I possessed only a polite mask. I put it on. "I'll do my best."

*Clang.*

The sound reverberated through the foyer and we all looked up at the ceiling.

"I saw the van in the drive. Do you have a new plumber?" The name on the side of the van had not been familiar.

Mother's lips thinned. "No. Of course not. Troy is out of town." Mother had used the same plumber, electrician, handyman, caterer, bartender, and florist since Methuselah walked the earth. God forbid any of them not be immediately available to her…"I'm not at all sure about this new man."

Thornton cleared his throat. "So, some excitement at your house, Ellison."

"That's one thing to call it."

"That decorator worked for us too. Cora couldn't pick out a decent paint color if her life depended on it. I guess now that the White woman is gone the kitchen will stay beige."

Cora's chin quivered. "She was very nice."

"She charged too much."

"Now, Thornton." Mother laid her hand on his arm. "You wouldn't want a bargain basement decorator."

*CLANG.*

A pained expression settled on Mother's face. "I hope he finishes soon. We have reservations." She adjusted her expression to don't-you-dare-argue. "The luncheon is Friday, so we'll be gathering here on Thursday evening. Put it on your calendar, Ellison."

Something landed on my head. I touched my hair and my fingers came away wet. I looked up at the ceiling. Another drip was forming. Oh dear. I stepped out of the way.

Mother looked up too. In fact, her gaze was riveted to the spot on the ceiling.

Drip, drip, drip.

"Cora, go get a bucket," said Thornton.

Too late. The drips swelled to a trickle.

*CLANG!*

The trickle swelled to a stream.

Mother's expression belonged in a horror movie.

"Where's the valve?" Not that I knew which way to turn the valve. "Can we turn off the water?"

"I don't know where it is." Unflappable Mother's voice was shrill.

"Well—" I looked at the only man in the front hall. Weren't men supposed to know about plumbing? "—someone should figure out the location." Quickly. The sound of the plumbing was Niagara Falls-esque.

The flow of water from the ceiling to Mother's Oriental swelled from stream to river.

Thornton, ever the man of action, strode to the bottom of the stairs and yelled, "Turn off the damn water."

Too little. Too late.

What happened next was inevitable.

The ceiling relocated to the floor, joined on its descent by a wall of water.

Mother, her St. John suit soaked, stood still as Lot's wife. So still, one might wonder if she had turned to salt. She hadn't, salt would've melted in the lake that was Mother's foyer. Mother was made of stronger stuff.

Cora wrung her hands.

Thornton picked a chunk of plaster from his wet hair and threw it on the sodden carpet. "This is a disaster, Frances. What are you going to do about Cora's benefactors' party?"

Mother shifted her horrified gaze from the ceiling to me. The idea flickered in her eyes then took hold. A conflagration of awful.

Sweet nine-pound baby Jesus. No! I shook my head. I held my hands up to ward off the inevitable. Please, no.

Mother, on fire with genius, ignored my distress. "That's not a problem. Ellison will host the party."

# SEVEN

I drove home damp with questionable water, sprinkled with bits of ceiling, and covered in a pall of impending disaster. A party? In two days?

A car I didn't recognize sat in the driveway. An AMC of some kind. An indeterminate shade of dark blue, the car looked fast sitting still. Hopefully whoever owned it would leave fast.

I parked my Triumph and got out.

Detective Peters and Anarchy climbed out of the other car.

Joy. Would it look suspicious if I hopped back in my car and drove away? Undoubtedly. Plus, they'd probably follow me.

I nodded at them, then a cold gust sent me scuttling for the front door. The wind probably seemed even colder because I was wet. *Brrr.* If the detectives wanted to talk to me, they could do it inside.

I pushed open the door and stepped into the warmth of my home and my dog's curious nose.

The police detectives followed me.

"What happened to you?" Anarchy's brows were drawn as if his concern was genuine.

I scratched Max's ears. "A ceiling mishap."

Detective Peters grunted. "We have a few more questions."

"No." The misery of damp clothes and an impending party gave me gumption I usually lacked.

"No?"

"No," I repeated. "I am wet. I am busy. And you did not call before you came. Now is not a convenient time for me to answer questions."

"This is a murder investigation." Peters leaned toward me and the scent of cheap cigars swirled under my nose.

Max growled softly. I patted his head. I could hold my own. Peters only thought he was intimidating. He wasn't. The rumpled detective wasn't in the same intimidation ballpark as Mother. With a well-chosen word (not even in person, she could be on the phone), Mother could terrorize a poor (relative term) young woman in the Junior League ghetto (cute young wives, cute starter homes, cute first children, and the cute first step on a path that led to being a social doyenne) into hosting a luncheon or chairing a fashion show. It didn't matter if the woman Mother was intimidating was eight months pregnant with triplets, she said yes. Mother never had to lean.

*Achoo.* "Pardon me."

Anarchy dug in a coat pocket, pulled out a handkerchief, and offered the folded bit of linen to me.

Peters scowled. "We need to verify timing."

I took Anarchy's hanky and wiped my nose. "The timing hasn't changed since the last time I told you. Now—" *achoo* "—if you gentlemen will excuse me, I'm going to go get out of these wet clothes."

Peters' wrinkled trench rustled when he crossed his arms. "We'll wait."

With that a quick shower became a leisurely bubble bath. "Suit yourself."

I climbed the steps with Max by my side.

"Ellison." Anarchy stopped me halfway to the second floor.

I looked over my shoulder.

Anarchy stared up at me, ignoring Detective Peters' black look. If the detective's thunderous demeanor was any indication, Anarchy was not supposed to call suspects by their first names.

"What?"

"You left when?" Anarchy asked.

"Five minutes after twelve. It's in my statement."

"And you returned?"

I climbed another step. "By twelve thirty."

"It doesn't take that long to drive to and from the grocery store," said Peters.

"It does if Aggie has car trouble and I run into someone I know in the parking lot."

"Who did you run into?" asked Anarchy. His voice sounded somehow brighter. "You didn't mention anyone earlier."

I hadn't?

"Mary Beth Brewer. She waited with Aggie until I got there."

"You know the Brewer woman well?" Something about the way Peters stood made me wary. Was he leaning on his toes? Leaning appeared to be a thing with him.

"Not *well*. But I've known her for years. What's the point in all this? You can't imagine Mary Beth had anything to do with the murder. She was at the store when Khaki was killed."

"She can corroborate your alibi," said Anarchy.

"I didn't know I needed corroboration."

"Everyone's alibi needs corroboration," said Detective Peters.

"Silly me." I searched Anarchy's face for some clue as to what was going on. Of course, he wore his cop face. The inscrutable one. The one that, unlike Detective Peters' leaning, could intimidate a suspect in half a heartbeat. But I wasn't really a suspect. Was I? "I thought Aggie and I provided alibis for each other."

Detective Peters grunted.

Anarchy said nothing.

Ugh. I resumed my climb. After all, I had a date with a long, luxurious bubble bath.

*Ding dong.*

The second floor was just steps away.

"I'll get that," said Peters.

I wished he wouldn't. "Really, you don't need to—"

He opened the door. "What?"

Unwelcome or not, that was not how guests were treated in my home. I descended the damned stairs.

Peters opened the door wider, allowing a chilly wind to sneak into the foyer. A chilly wind and Preston George. "Ellison," he said. "May I have a word?"

I stared at the latest addition to my foyer. My jaw *might* have dropped an inch or two. Over the course of my whole life, nothing like this had happened before. My friends' husbands didn't pop over for a chat.

"Is Jinx all right?"

He jerked his chin. "She's fine." Preston took in my ensemble—wet sweater, wet slacks, wet hair, and a sprinkling of plaster. "Are you?"

"I'm fine." I glanced at the detectives, both of whom seemed content to let Preston and me continue our scintillating conversation uninterrupted. "Now's not the most convenient time."

"This is important."

Detective Peters grumbled. Apparently nothing Preston might say was as important as a murder investigation.

"I can come by your office in the morning." Dammit. I'd been raised to keep men happy, not placating an unhappy one was harder than expected. I didn't actually want to talk to Preston. There were rules. No white after Labor Day. Never arrive early for a dinner party. Don't get involved in your friends' marriages. The man your friend couldn't wait to divorce today was tomorrow's version of forever, and the friend who'd been picking up crumpled tissue and commiserating about what a louse he was finds herself in the role of villain. "Actually, now that I think about it, the next two days are crazy for me. Maybe next week?"

"Tomorrow. Nine o'clock."

"I'm really very busy."

"Please?"

How did he fill one word with so much pain?

"I—"

*Ding dong.*

I glanced at my watch. Was that the time?

Again, Detective Peters opened the door.

Hunter Tafft stood on the other side. His gaze traveled from

Preston (he nodded) to Anarchy and Detective Peters (his lips thinned) to me (his eyes widened). "I'll call and change our reservation."

An hour later I sat across from Hunter at a small table covered in crisp white linen. "I don't see how I can get out of it." I lifted the wine glass to my lips and drank. Deeply.

Across from me, Hunter rubbed his chin. "Tell her it's unseemly to have a party on Thursday when someone was murdered in the house on Monday."

"I tried that. Mother has no ceiling in her front entry. She's willing to overlook the niceties."

Around us, the small restaurant was filled with people who weren't being forced to host a cocktail party in two days.

I took another sip. "She needs help and she's my mother. What else can I do?"

A waiter appeared next to our table.

"Have we decided?"

"Lemon chicken with capers." I handed him the menu.

"The same," said Hunter.

"Would we like to start with a salad?"

Was he joining us? Nurses and waiters and the royal *we*. I looked up from my wine glass, a rude retort primed on my lips.

"The house salad for both of us."

The waiter nodded and left us.

I glared at Hunter.

He pursed his lips as if he was battling a smile. "I realize you've had a long day, but lambasting a waiter won't help. And he might spit in our food before he brings it to us."

He was right. As usual. Most annoying.

I looked away.

Across the restaurant, Mary Beth Brewer was dining with another woman, one whose back was to me. Odd. Mary Beth's husband always struck me as the dinner-on-the-table-at-six-thirty type, not the my-wife-can-go-out-for-dinner-with-friends-on-a-Tuesday type.

Mary Beth said something to her dinner companion, rose, and approached our table.

Hunter stood.

"Please don't get up." Mary Beth smiled at Hunter.

He ignored her request. "How nice to see you, Mary Beth."

The dim mood-lighting did nothing to hide the sudden flush on her cheeks. "Please sit." She shifted her attention to me. "I just can't believe what happened after I saw you yesterday. You're all right?"

"Fine."

"Poor Khaki." The color of her cheeks deepened. Dollars to donuts she'd just remembered poor Khaki was once married to the man standing next to her. "She did some work for me."

"Oh?"

"She was very good." Mary Beth added an earnest nod. "Very good."

"So many people hired her. She must have been." Although, I couldn't name one home, or even one room, that said *designed by Khaki White*. She might have been good, but she wasn't distinctive.

"Your housekeeper? Did you get her car working?"

"We bought her a new one."

Hunter, who'd been looking mildly bored, focused his gaze on me. My cheeks, traitorous bits of flesh, warmed.

"How nice." Mary Beth glanced over her shoulder at her waiting friend. "I won't keep you from your dinner."

"Lovely to see you, Mary Beth," said Hunter.

I murmured something similar.

Mary Beth returned to her table.

Hunter sat. "You bought Aggie a car?"

"I did."

He blinked.

"You could have called me."

"So you could buy the car? She works for me."

"But—"

"But what? Women can buy cars. The salesman only asked twice if I needed to check with my husband." The man had worried the knot of his tie, smoothed his hair, and even mumbled something about calling his manager. "I think he felt better when I told him I was a widow."

"I'll pay for half."

"No. Aggie is the best thing that has ever happened to Grace and me. If I want to buy her a car, I will."

We might have argued more, but the waiter arrived with our salads. Amidst the placing of plates and offering of fresh ground pepper, it occurred to me that I'd liked buying Aggie her car. Not just because it made her happy but because I could. A major purchase and I didn't have to consult anyone. It was...empowering.

The waiter departed with a promise to return and top off our water glasses.

I stabbed a blameless bit of romaine. "This isn't working."

"What's not working?"

"This." The man sitting across from me could make middle-aged women blush with just a glance (including me), but I wasn't ready for another man to tell me what to do, or how to spend my money. "Us."

Hunter put his salad fork down on the edge of his plate.

I put my fork down too. "There are plenty of women who'd trade their eye-teeth for your attention. You should date one of them."

"I don't want one of them. I want you." His voice was velvet.

Precisely the kind of words said in precisely the kind of tone that could leave a woman breathless. I dragged air into my lungs and straightened my spine. "I'm nearly forty and I've only been alive for a few months."

He tilted his head slightly. Amused or annoyed? "So being with me would be akin to death."

Annoyed.

I reclaimed my fork. I needed *something* to hold onto. "I don't mean you per say. I mean any man. I need to find out what it's like to be on my own before I can be with anyone." Not that I'd be alive to find out. As soon as Mother found out I'd given Hunter Tafft walking papers, she'd kill me.

"You've said this before. I told you, I'd wait."

Hunter's idea of waiting was dinners and dances and (God help me) kisses. Did he not see the problem? "I just can't. I—" Why was Pete Brewer shoving the maître d'?

"Get the hell out of my way."

Every head in the restaurant turned. Including Mary Beth's. Her eyes widened. Her cheeks paled.

The woman she was dining with stood. Turned. Sally Broome. The only female divorce attorney in town. Not a friendly dinner. Business.

Pete pushed past the maître d', leaned over Mary Beth's table, and said, "You're coming home. Now."

"I take it you got the papers?" Sally sounded cool and unflustered. Remarkably so given that Pete had clenched his hands into fists, his cheeks were the color of old brick, and fire seemed to be shooting from his eyes.

"Bitch."

Sally brushed a bit of lint off the sleeve of her blouse. "She's not going home with you."

Mary Beth gripped the edge of the table. "I'm not. We're done, Pete."

"I'm sorry. It won't happen again. I swear."

A tear trickled down Mary Beth's cheek. "But it does. You promise and then—I just can't do this anymore."

Pete's head swiveled, casting equal glares upon his wife and her lawyer. "You won't get a dime." His gaze landed on Sally. "She doesn't have two cents. She can't pay you."

Sally glanced around the restaurant and realized she had a rapt audience. "Your marriage is over."

"Bitch." Pete needed some new material.

Hunter and I glanced at each other. This was awful. Poor Mary

Beth. And Pete, when he regained control of his temper, would be mortified.

Hunter leaned toward me. "I'll get him out of here. I take it you can cover dinner?" Was there a touch of acerbity in Hunter's tone?

I nodded.

Hunter stood and strode across the restaurant. "Pete!" He pounded Brewer on the back. "This isn't the time or the place. Let's you and me go get a drink."

Pete stopped trying to kill Sally Broome with his gaze and looked at Hunter.

Hunter said something too quiet for me to hear and Pete nodded. Slowly. His ruddy cheeks paled. Maybe he'd noticed the rapt faces around him. Or maybe Hunter told him his little outburst was going to cost him big in divorce court.

Either way, he took a step away from the table. "Yeah. Sure."

With Hunter at his side, he turned and left.

No one spoke. The stunned hush was deafening.

With a shaking hand, Mary Beth reached for her wine, knocked over her water glass, and burst into tears.

Sally Broome went to her, draped her arm around Mary Beth's shoulders, and whispered something, presumably comforting, in her ear.

Someone at another table spoke.

A woman I didn't know approached Mary Beth's table and offered a handkerchief.

I threw a few bills on the table, went to Mary Beth, and knelt beside her. "If you need anything—anything—call."

She nodded and mopped her eyes with the borrowed hanky.

Sally Broome settled her gaze on me. "Mrs. Russell, please give Mr. Tafft my thanks. Without him, this scene could have been much worse."

"I will." Dammit. I couldn't even break up with Hunter without him being chivalrous.

# EIGHT

I sent Grace off to school and sat down for some serious one-on-one time with Mr. Coffee.

"What a mess," I said.

Mr. Coffee was the strong, silent type. He didn't answer. Nor did he disagree.

He couldn't disagree. When I woke up on Monday morning, finding a body and hosting a benefactors' party had not figured in my calculations for the week. Nor had a visit to Preston George's office.

Preston manufactured something—air filters or heating coils or casings for furnaces. I never could remember what. It was a nice solid company with nice solid returns. Respectable. Dependable. Not sexy. Rather like Preston. There are things one can manufacture that are not so respectable, that are slightly—or not so slightly—embarrassing. Just look at my brother-in-law, the rubber king of Ohio. And no, not tires or galoshes or pencil erasers. Preston had taken the slightly less profitable but far more socially acceptable route and made—I scrunched my face and thought hard—a component for air conditioners.

"I ought to get dressed. I have to leave soon."

Mr. Coffee didn't reply but his half-full pot glistened in the morning sun.

"You're right. One more cup." I poured.

My thoughts crept down the hall and peeked into Henry's study. Who had murdered Khaki? Who wanted her dead? Everyone I'd talked to, with the exception of Jinx, liked Khaki. Granted that might be because she was dead and people tended to turn dead people into saints, but...

I pushed away from the kitchen counter and followed my thoughts down the hall.

Max lifted his sleepy head off his paws but opted not to come with me.

Khaki had let someone into the house. Someone who drove a white Mercedes? She'd walked back to Henry's study, turned to face the door, and they'd shot her. It seemed a cold-blooded, almost clinical way to kill someone. No anger, no passion, just pressure on a trigger. Why hadn't they killed her by the front door? Had they followed her and taken something from her enormous tote bag? Did she have a chance to plead for her life before the killer put a bullet in her brain?

I opened the door to the study. It was all there. The dark paneling, the heavy furniture, the hideous carpet. The only thing missing was Khaki.

I shuddered, an involuntary reaction that shook my teeth. Then I shook my shoulders. On purpose. As if I could shake off the brutality of Khaki's death.

I glanced again into the dust-covered study. There was no way we could clean it up and get the house ready for a party. We'd have to keep it closed off on Thursday night—not that anyone was ghoulish enough to want to drink cocktails where Khaki died. I hoped they weren't. They were. We'd have to keep the study locked.

I pulled the door closed a shade too hard, trudged up the front steps, threw on a wrap dress and a pair of pumps, ran a comb through my hair, and powdered my nose.

Ready. Except I had no idea what to say to Preston. *Were you sleeping with Khaki?* That seemed a bit blunt as an opening. *Did you kill her?* More so. Also dangerous if he actually had. *Did Jinx kill her?* That was downright rude.

I descended the stairs.

Max ambled into the foyer to check up on me.

"Behave."

He yawned.

"Aggie will be here soon."

He rubbed his grey head against my leg and I scratched behind his ear. "How did a killer get past you?"

Max kept his own counsel.

I bent, dropped a kiss on the top of his head, grabbed my Gucci trench coat out of the hall closet, put it on, and slipped out the front door.

November had taken hold. Leaden skies, cold wind, and a raw quality to the air that promised early, heavy snow. The weather matched my mood.

I slipped into the driver's seat and pointed the car toward the industrial district where Preston kept his office.

The grey of the concrete, the chain link fence, and the ugly building were every bit as depressing as the sky. Surely Preston could afford a nicer office?

I parked and walked across the gritty pavement.

My coat wasn't near enough protection against the wind. I pulled the collar up and longed for a hat.

The scents of steel and oil welcomed me to Preston's building. That was all that did. I stood in a dingy front office—pea soup carpet, a lone desk, and faded paint. A woman held a phone to her ear. She nodded at me and held up a single finger.

I waited. Standing. Unwilling to subject my new coat to whatever stained the chairs pushed against the wall.

She hung up the phone and clipped an earring on her lobe. "May I help you?"

"I'm not sure I'm in the right place. I have an appointment with Preston. Mr. George. Is this his business?"

"It is." She raised a brow that had been plucked to near extinction. "You don't seem the type."

The type? "Be that as it may, would you please tell him that Ellison Russell is here?"

She pulled off her earring, picked up the phone, and pushed one of the buttons at the bottom of the device. "Ellison Russell here to see Mr. George." She hung up the phone and waved toward the questionable chairs. "You can have a seat. His secretary will be right out."

"If you don't mind, I'll stand."

"Suit yourself." She replaced her earring and turned her attention to a typewriter. Although, how she hoped to type with the frosted pink talons at the end of her fingers was beyond me.

Hunt-and-peck.

Hunt-and-peck.

As chilly as it was outside, it was stuffy inside. I unbuttoned my coat and loosened the belt.

The receptionist completed a word and looked up. "You want some coffee?"

"Thank you, that would be lovely."

"You ain't tasted it yet."

Oh dear. It couldn't be any worse than Marian's, could it? I glanced again at the ugly carpet and decided the coffee could be worse. I'd expected something...nicer. Did Preston actually make any money from this place?

The receptionist grabbed the edge of her desk and pushed herself out of her chair. She limped to a coffeemaker in the corner and poured what looked like motor oil into a Styrofoam cup.

She limped back to me. "Here you go."

I took the cup from her hands and she returned to her desk, sitting with a grunt.

"Are you all right?"

"Me? Old injury. I had a mishap with a flight of stairs. Twice."

"Twice?"

She squinted at the paper in her typewriter, swore softly, then looked up at me. "I was lucky it wasn't three times."

A woman with a crooked nose, pursed lips, and a sweater set the color of Pepto-Bismol opened a door to the front office. "Mr. George will see you now."

Clutching my cup of motor oil, I followed her down a long hallway to an elevator. She pressed the up button and glanced at the cup in my hand. "I wouldn't drink that if I were you. Sheri can't make coffee to save her life. We have decent stuff upstairs."

"Thank you." I followed her onto a paneled elevator.

The doors slid closed, the car lurched, and we rose.

When the elevator doors opened, she stepped into another hallway and turned right. "This way."

She led me through a small office. "Let me take that for you." She held out her hand.

I relinquished Sheri's coffee without regret.

She tapped on an oak door, waited a few seconds, then opened it. "Mr. George, here's Mrs. Russell for you."

Preston rose from his desk chair.

I stepped inside.

"I'll be back with fresh coffee." Preston's secretary closed the door behind her, leaving me to take stock of Preston's office. Three walls were lined waist-high with manuals that probably required an engineering degree to decipher. The fourth wall was glass with a view of the factory floor. And then there was the Stella. The painting hung above the manuals on the west wall.

"Good morning, Preston." I crossed the room, studied. "From his Protractor Series."

"Yes." He stepped out from behind his desk. "Thank you for coming." He waved at a chair that didn't look...sticky. "Please have a seat."

I slipped off my coat.

"I'll take that." He took the trench from my hands and hung it on a coat tree.

Henry used to say you could tell a lot about a man from his office. What did Preston's office say? There were manuals, there was a view of the factory floor, there was the Stella, and there were pictures of Jinx on the credenza. Lots of them. The office said Preston was a hard-working engineer who appreciated good art and loved his wife.

Appearances could be deceiving.

I sat, crossed my hands in my lap, and waited.

Preston resumed his seat behind the desk, arranged a few pens in perfect alignment, and cleared his throat.

Tap, tap.

"Yes." He sounded grateful for the interruption, as if we'd been having an uncomfortable conversation rather than sitting in awkward silence.

The office door opened. "I have Mrs. Russell's coffee." Preston's secretary brought a porcelain mug instead of a Styrofoam cup.

"Thank you."

"You're welcome." She departed, leaving Preston to stare at his pens and me to stare at his Stella.

I sipped.

He shifted in his chair.

I sat back and studied the flow of lines across the canvas. Preston had brought me here. He could tell me what he wanted. Much as I'd dearly love to ask him about Khaki, I wasn't about to help him by starting a conversation.

He cleared his throat and ringed the inside of his collar as if his shirt was suddenly too tight. Since his collar was open, that was an impossibility.

I crossed my ankles.

He steepled his fingers and held them in front of his face, covering his mouth and nose. "This is difficult."

"I think it's like ripping off a Band-Aid, better if you do it quickly." Better for me.

He lowered his head until I saw the crown, barely covered by thinning hair. "Jinx believes I was having an affair with Khaki. She's carrying on with the tennis pro to get back at me."

So he knew. "Were you?"

He looked up. "Was I what?"

"Having an affair with Khaki."

"No." His answer was immediate and forceful—totally believable—but my extensive experience with a cheating spouse had taught me that men were excellent liars.

"Then tell Jinx."

"She won't believe me."

"Why not?"

"Khaki and I were working on a project together. It required some late nights."

Preston manufactured a highly engineered part for air conditioners. I glanced at the technical manuals and was less certain about the parts part. Maybe he made air conditioners. Khaki had carried around fabric swatches. "What project?"

"I can't tell you."

Why was I here if he couldn't tell me anything? "Can you tell Jinx?"

He deflated like a pricked balloon. "My wife is the best thing that ever happened to me. She's my lodestone." He clasped his hands and rested them on the desk. "And she can't keep a secret."

He was not wrong. Jinx loved a good story. Especially if she was one of the first people to tell it. "Tell her that. The lodestone part." Surely he was smart enough not to tell Jinx he thought she gossiped too much.

"I've told her that a million times. She wants to know what Khaki and I were doing, and I can't tell her." The poor man sounded miserable. The corners of his mouth drooped. Furrows cut into his forehead.

So it was Khaki's secret? "Khaki doesn't care if you tell anyone." It was a harsh thing to say. Harsh but true. Khaki stopped caring when someone shot her.

"It wasn't Khaki's secret either."

I took a sip of coffee. Not up to Mr. Coffee's standards but not motor oil. Khaki and Preston had kept a secret. What was it? Whose was it? "You know, Preston, Khaki was killed for a reason. Maybe you should tell the police."

He paled. "I can't." He shook his head. "I could go to jai—" He rubbed his eyes and fell silent.

People backed themselves into corners all the time. Preston seemed to have wedged himself in tightly. He had a secret he couldn't share with his wife or the police. Now Jinx was having an affair and Khaki had been murdered. And his solution was me?

"What do you want me to do, Preston?"

"You've got to tell Jinx that Khaki and I weren't having an affair."

"Won't do a whit of good." Did he really think Jinx would be placated with that? "You've got to tell her this secret. Tell her what's going on."

"I can't." He dropped his head to his hands. "Please. Just tell Jinx." His voice cracked as he said his wife's name.

I had a terrible, awful feeling that Preston might sob. "All right. I'll tell her." What else could I say? The last thing in the world I wanted was to watch a grown man cry. "But Preston, I think you're faced with a choice. Keep your secret or keep your marriage." I leaned forward and put the coffee mug on the edge of his crowded desk. "Do you know why Khaki was murdered?"

"No!" Too forceful. Too quick.

I raised a brow and waited.

He stood, jack-in-the-box quick. "Thank you for coming." If ever there was a hint to leave...

"If you want me to talk to Jinx, tell me what's going on. I *can* keep a secret."

Preston opened and closed his mouth. Twice. He fiddled with his collar again. He glanced down at the desk and straightened an already straight pen. "I'm sorry I wasted your time." He emerged from behind his desk, took my coat off the tree, and held it for me.

I stood but made no move to slide my arms into the coat's sleeves. "She was murdered. She deserves justice."

"Goodbye, Ellison."

"Do you know who killed her?"

His eyes widened and his cheeks paled. "No."

Maybe he was telling the truth. Maybe he didn't know for certain. But I'd bet my Gucci trench he had a pretty good guess. "Preston—"

He handed me my coat.

"I have another appointment, Ellison. Thank you again." He turned his back on me.

"Preston." He paused on his walk back to his desk. Paused but didn't turn. I spoke to the muted plaid of his sport coat. "Be careful. Someone shot Khaki in cold blood. If you know something, you could be next."

# NINE

If I'd known I'd find Mother at my house, I'd have taken a detour via St. Louis. Or, more apropos, Omaha.

After all, Mother would make a wonderful Marlin Perkins...*go fight that lion, Jim—*

*I mean, Ellison.*

I opened the front door and found her directing Penelope, her housekeeper, and Frank, her houseman. Under Mother's watchful eye, Penelope perched atop a stepladder like some long-suffering bird and ran a feather duster over the chandelier. Frank was on his hands and knees hunting nonexistent dust bunnies. Max, his head tilted slightly to the side, watched.

"What are you doing?" My voice was as chilly and unwelcoming as the weather outside.

"Helping you." Mother held up a legal pad filled with her elegant script.

"I didn't ask for help." I grabbed and held the wobbly ladder. "Penelope, get down from there."

Penelope looked at Mother who shook her head.

The housekeeper continued dusting.

Dammit.

I shifted my gaze to the houseman with his cheek pressed to the floor. "There's not a speck of dust under that chest. Get up, Frank."

Frank stood—slowly, the man was sixty-five if he was a day, not to mention the arthritis in his knees. He had no business crawling around on the floor. He glanced at Mother's aggrieved expression and manufactured an apology. "I'm sorry, Mrs. Walford, but's she's right. No dust. It's as clean as your house."

Mother snorted.

"Where is Aggie?" I demanded. Did Mother have her cleaning light sockets with a screwdriver?

"She is polishing silver in the kitchen." Mother added some starch to her tone.

The silver? Since it was polished just last week, that task had figured rather low on the to-do list Aggie and I had written.

I clenched my jaw and forced a smile for Penelope and Frank's benefit. "May I speak with you in the living room?"

Mother didn't move.

"Please?" I let go of the ladder (Penelope had made her choice, she could live with the consequences) and marched toward my spotlessly clean living room. Mother damned well better follow me, or I'd tell her just what I thought of her unannounced arrival in front of the help. Perhaps she sensed that. After a few seconds, her heels clicked behind me.

She stepped inside and I closed the door.

*Ten, nine, eight, seven...*

She tapped her list with the tip of her fingernail. I was wasting time.

"How dare you?" The words came out in a rush. So much for calming breaths and counting down from ten. "How. Dare. You?"

Her eyes widened as if she had no earthly clue what I meant. "What are you talking about, dear?"

"Your staff in my foyer."

"Oh. That." She waved an elegant wrist toward the closed door. "They're helping."

She was interfering and she knew it. I wasn't buying her wide-eyed innocent act for a second. "No, Mother. You're interfering."

She narrowed her eyes.

I practically shook with emotion I didn't care to name. "Helping would be calling and asking if I needed help. Helping would be offering to call the caterer, and the florist, and the bartender. Helping would be asking if you could run errands. That—" I pointed at the door "—is not helping. That is your way of telling me my house isn't clean enough for your friends."

"Are you quite finished?" With her narrowed eyes, pale cheeks, and helmet of white hair, she looked like a general ready to decimate her enemies. Namely me.

*Scratch.*

I opened the door.

Max walked inside and stood beside me, his shoulder pressed against my leg. At least I had one ally in this battle I couldn't hope to win. I scratched behind his ear and closed the door.

"You're being unreasonable, Ellison."

"Really? If Aggie and I showed up at your house with a to-do list longer than the fairway on the seventeenth hole, you'd be delighted?"

"Don't be ridiculous." Her tone frosted the windows.

"I'm not."

We glared at each other. Mother waiting for me to cede, to apologize, to do as she asked.

That wasn't happening.

Max whined softly. *Was I okay?*

Without interrupting our staring match, I stroked the top of his head.

"There's an order to things," she said.

I glanced around my immaculate living room and raised a brow.

"Order is all we have."

"Pardon me?"

"Chaos is out there. Waiting." She pointed at the window. "Drugs and sex and ugly divorce. We need order to keep chaos at bay."

What this had to do with asking an arthritic man to crawl around on the floor looking for dust bunnies, I did not know.

"Don't roll your eyes at me, young lady."

"I'm not fifteen anymore, and you are in the wrong."

"I most certainly am not. Whether you choose to recognize it or not, there is an order to our lives. A husband. Children. A nice home. Making a difference in the community. These are the things that give our lives meaning. They keep chaos at bay. Cleaning house for a party keeps chaos at bay."

"Mother." My voice was softer than I intended. Did she really believe that cleaning my house would make everything right in the world?

"Do you remember the story of the three little pigs?"

Max and I both tilted our heads. Had Mother been inhaling cleaning fluid?

"The first little pig built his house of straw and the wolf blew it down. The second used twigs and the wolf was able to blow it away. But the third pig—" she pointed a finger at me (a change from pointing her finger at her numbered list) "—the third pig used brick, and no matter how hard he tried, the wolf couldn't destroy that house."

In Mother's mind, a husband, children, a nice—very clean—home, and a place in society were the equivalent of a brick house? They kept the wolf from the door?

She was wrong. So very, very wrong.

The wolf found a way inside. Always. Husbands cheated. So did wives. Children did drugs or dropped out of school. People were murdered in the study. And that nice offer to help a charity turned around and bit you in the ass.

She was clinging to a fairy tale.

"It doesn't work that way, Mother."

"It does." She closed her eyes and her knuckles whitened around the edge of her to-do list. She bit her lip. "It does."

For one crazy, horrific moment I thought she might cry.

Instead, she opened her eyes (no tears—instead, they blazed like a zealot's) and shook her list at me. "This party is a reflection on me. You are a reflection on me."

"I am a reflection on myself, not you."

"Don't be naïve." This from a woman who thought a clean house could keep the wolves at bay?

The sound of a car door closing drew both our gazes to the window. Anarchy and Detective Peters stood in the drive looking up at the house. The aged brick and crisp white trim failed to charm them. They both wore grim expressions.

"Damn. Again?" Mother said what I was thinking. Then she added, "With order in your life, this sort of thing wouldn't happen." By *order*, she meant Hunter Tafft. Perhaps now was not the best time to mention we'd gone our separate ways. At my behest.

The two men walked out of our line of sight.

*Ding dong.*

"Tell them we're getting ready for a party and you simply don't have time to talk to them."

Because telling a homicide detective that planning a party was more important than the woman murdered in my home would go over so well.

With that bit of horrifically bad advice, Mother opened the door to the foyer and slipped away.

I waited next to the fireplace. Too bad there wasn't a fire burning. My hands could do with some warmth. Max would have enjoyed it too.

*Tap, tap.*

"Come in."

Anarchy stepped into the living room, closing the door behind him. "What's going on out there?"

"Mother."

"She decided to clean your house?"

"That pretty much sums it up. The ceiling in her foyer collapsed so she volunteered me to host a cocktail party on Thursday night."

Anarchy digested that bit of news while Max meandered over to say *hello.*

"No one will go in the study. I'll keep the door locked."

Our gazes met and I saw sympathy in his eyes. He knew

standing up to Mother was like standing up to a hurricane. Generally—always—a bad idea. "Be sure that you do."

"What can I help you with?" I asked.

"We've been looking into Mrs. White's relationships." He bent and scratched under Max's chin.

My thoughts raced back to Preston and Jinx.

"There's some indication that Mrs. White was up to something illicit."

"You mean an affair?"

His coffee brown gaze returned to me. "No. Was she having an affair?"

Why couldn't I keep my big mouth closed? "Not that I know of." Not exactly a lie. I didn't *have* to scratch the end of my nose. "What was Khaki up to?"

Anarchy glanced down at the Persian rug that covered the living room floor. "How much would you expect to pay for a Heriz runner?"

"Authentic?"

His upper lip twitched as if I'd amused him. "Of course."

"Museum quality?"

"Probably not. But close."

I pondered. "A thousand dollars give or take."

"And if it was museum quality?"

"I don't know. Twice that? Why?"

"One of Mrs. White's clients recently took a rug in for repair. Their dog chewed off the fringe. They had the rug appraised while it was at the shop. It was worth about half of what they paid."

"Decorators overcharge all the time." It might've been unethical, but it wasn't illicit.

"When we looked up that rug in Mrs. White's books, she showed a twenty percent markup."

I sat down in one of the wingbacks that flanked the fireplace. "Please, sit." I nodded to the second chair. "Khaki sold a thousand-dollar rug for two thousand but listed the sale as twelve hundred?"

Anarchy sat across from me. "That's about right."

"What happened to the eight hundred dollars?"

"That's what we'd like to know. We're looking for the money." He wore his cop expression—serious, focused, hard.

"Why are you telling me this?"

"Did she quote you any prices?"

"No. Monday was the first time she'd come to the house."

"So you don't know if she planned on overcharging you?"

"I don't see how she could. I wasn't interested in buying a carpet, and even if I was, I know what they cost."

"Do most women know how much a rug like that costs?"

"I don't know. The only reason I do is because Max ate half the upstairs runner when he was a puppy." I scowled at my dog who didn't act remotely guilty (then again, he never did). "I had to replace it."

I glanced at my hands. Did Anarchy really think that bilking her clients had gotten Khaki killed? "If someone overcharged me and I found out about it, I'd sue them not kill them."

"You'd tell everyone you knew, right?"

It was true. If a decorator fleeced me or any of my friends like that, she'd be the talk of every bridge table in town. "Yes."

"All the women who've used Mrs. White speak highly of her." He glanced again at the rug. "Even when we've pointed out that she overcharged."

"What did their husbands say?"

A shadow crossed over his face. "They were less flattering."

Of course they were. It was their money.

A few seconds passed in silence.

Anarchy leaned back. "That's a pretty dress to clean house in."

Those brown eyes of his didn't miss much. And right now, those eyes were looking more like melting chocolate and less like forged steel.

I shifted in my chair and pulled at the hem of my dress. Did he mean that as a compliment or was he pointing out that I wasn't actually doing any work? "I had an appointment this morning."

"With whom?"

"No one important." I scrambled for a new topic. One that didn't include my dress, Jinx, or Preston and Khaki's secret project. "Where's Detective Peters?"

"He's with Aggie. He had some questions about Hunter Tafft." His voice flattened when he said Hunter's name.

I smiled. I couldn't help it. Aggie was endlessly loyal to the man who paid her late husband's medical bills. "He expects Aggie to answer them?"

"Hope springs eternal." Dry as Saharan sand—that was his tone.

"How did you and Detective Peters become partners?"

"It's been in the works for a while now. Peters' last partner took early retirement."

"What about your last partner?" I'd never seen Anarchy with another cop. Had he even had a partner?

"I take some getting used to."

"How so?"

"Most of the men on the force—their fathers were cops. It's like a family business."

"And your father's a professor."

"You remember that?" His brown gaze warmed me. Good thing there wasn't a fire in the hearth. The way Anarchy was looking at me combined with an open flame would have melted me into a puddle.

"I do." There wasn't much I forgot about Anarchy Jones.

"Also, I went to college. Most of the men on the force have not."

"Where did you go? Berkley?" His father was a professor at Berkley.

"No." For the first time since I'd met him, Anarchy fidgeted. He shifted in his chair. He pinched the pleat in his pants. He glanced out the window. "Stanford." His voice was so low I almost missed hearing him.

Stanford. If one could look past the ugly plaid of his sport coat, there was more to Anarchy than met the eye. "What did you study?"

Now he glanced at the ceiling. "History and English. I planned on going to law school."

"Why didn't you?"

A grin flashed across his face. "To some, the only thing worse than being a lawyer is being a cop."

I had to ask. "Who is some?"

His face—always lean, always hard—looked downright harsh. "My father."

"So you're a cop to annoy your dad?"

He shook his head. "I'm a cop because I like rules."

You don't say.

"Rules need to be enforced," he continued. "And I like to think I'm making a difference. Helping people."

"What do the other officers on the force think about Stanford?"

"I've been on the job for a long time."

He hadn't answered my question. Maybe he wouldn't. Although, I'd learned more about Anarchy in the last five minutes than I had in the previous five months. Sharing personal information wasn't exactly high on his priority list. If I repeated the question, would he return to his taciturn ways? I waited.

He rubbed his chin. "They thought I was playing and they resented me."

"And now?" Low, barely there words.

His eyes twinkled. "Now they just resent me."

"Does Peters resent you?"

"You'd have to ask Peters."

"Ask me what?"

I'd been so wrapped up in listening to Anarchy, I hadn't noticed him come in.

My hands fluttered like a debutante's.

"If you've decided on a prime suspect." Anarchy saved me from a bumbling lie.

Detective Peters scratched his cheek (maybe it wouldn't itch if he did a better job shaving). "We've timed it out. Tafft couldn't have done it." He scowled. "I supposed you'll call him and tell him that."

"That he didn't kill Khaki? He already knows."

Detective Peters' eyebrows lowered and the skin around his eyes scrunched. He looked like a cross between Dirty Harry and Oscar the Grouch. "You have no alibi."

"I was picking up Aggie."

"And we have only your word that Mrs. White was alive when you left." The man was delusional.

"Peters—" Anarchy crossed his arms and tilted his head as if he was trying to figure out how his partner had come up with me as a suspect. "Mrs. Russell didn't kill anyone."

"So says you." More Dirty Harry less Oscar the Grouch. He squinted at me. "We're keeping an eye on you, Mrs. Russell."

"You'll find me very boring."

"Hmph." He shoved his hands in his pockets. Was he fingering his cuffs? "Don't leave town."

# TEN

Somehow I got Mother out of the house. Somehow. My scowl? Doubtful. Not even when paired with crossed arms. The promise to talk about dead bodies at the party if she didn't leave? Bingo. It was the threat of discussing bodies that got her out of my foyer and returned her to her car.

Aggie and I breathed deep sighs.

Max returned to his favorite spot in the kitchen for a she's-out-of-the-house-and-I-don't-have-to-watch-her-anymore nap.

Aggie held up Mr. Coffee's pot. "Shall I make fresh?"

"Please."

Aggie poured out the old coffee, rinsed the pot, and refilled Mr. Coffee's reservoir.

A single pair of silver candlesticks stood on the kitchen island. They'd belonged to my great-grandmother, weighed three tons, and were shiny enough to make me squint.

"That's the silver you polished?"

Aggie nodded. "I did. Then I went back to our list."

"What needs to be done?" Guilt niggled at me. I had a bridge game scheduled, and I hadn't even tried to find a sub. When I departed, Aggie would be left with the entire list.

"Not much. The house is pretty much party-ready all the time. The caterer is bringing the food tomorrow. The rental company will drop off plates and glassware later today." She glanced at her watch. "In an hour or so. The liquor store delivers around three. The florist is scheduled for two o'clock tomorrow. And the harpist won't arrive until an hour before the party."

"The harpist?" Mother hired a harpist?

"Yes." There was no judgment in Aggie's voice.

"A harpist." There was plenty of judgment in mine. "Why not a jazz trio?"

Aggie knew I didn't expect an answer. "I'll put these in the dining room." She picked up the candlesticks and disappeared.

With a charming gurgle followed by a steamy sigh, Mr. Coffee finished filling his pot.

I poured myself a cup, stared into its depths, and thought about bridge. Of my foursome, Jinx always arrived early, I arrived on time, and Libba and Daisy arrived late. If I arrived early, I'd be able to recount my visit with Preston to Jinx. But did I want to? Clichéd cuddling with the tennis pro aside, she was one of my dearest friends. Getting involved in her marriage was a bad idea.

But Preston had begged.

Like Mr. Coffee, I sighed. Unlike Mr. Coffee, my sigh wasn't filled with promise. The sigh escaping my lips sank to the floor and slinked past Aggie's ankles on its way out the door.

Aggie stood in the doorway, her forehead puckered with concern. "Are you okay?"

A second sigh joined the first. "Preston George wants me to tell Jinx he hasn't been cheating on her."

"Has he?"

"I don't think so."

"Then you should tell her."

Aggie made telling Jinx sound so easy. An hour later, sitting alone in the card room and drumming my fingers against the table, telling Jinx didn't seem easy. Instead, telling her struck me as difficult. *You know that tennis pro you've been boffing to get even with your husband? You might want to stop, because your husband wasn't having an affair.* Who wants to hear that?

"You're here early." Jinx claimed the chair next to me by hanging her purse on its back. "What's the occasion?"

"I was in Aggie's way. She's getting ready for the party Mother moved to my house."

"That's right. My mother is attending. She said something about Frances having a plumbing issue."

"Her ceiling fell on us."

"That must have been fun." Jinx did sarcasm well.

"Almost as much fun as finding a body." To wit, no fun at all.

We both thought about Khaki's lifeless body staring sightlessly at the ceiling in the study. At least I did.

"Do the police have any leads as to who killed Khaki?" Jinx had been thinking about her too.

"No." And since Jinx had mentioned Khaki by name, avoiding telling her about my conversation with Preston would be cowardly. It was also tempting. I picked up a deck of cards and shuffled. "I went by Preston's office this morning."

Her brows rose. Her eyes glittered. "Oh?"

"He asked me to come."

Jinx's brows rose higher.

"He wants me to convince you he wasn't having an affair with Khaki."

She snorted softly. "And you believed him?"

"I did. I do."

"If they weren't having an affair, what were they doing all those nights?"

"He said they were working on a project."

Jinx snorted loudly.

I didn't blame her. Preston's explanation was remarkably weak.

She reached over and patted my hand. "I know you're only trying to help, but this is between Preston and me." Translation: *butt out.*

"I really did believe him, Jinx. He loves you."

"Easy for him to say."

"I think he meant it."

The tips of her nails dug into the back of my hand and the expression in her grey eyes was as cold as concrete in January. I shivered.

We said nothing. I was still thinking of Khaki's sightless eyes. Lord only knew what Jinx was thinking about. How much pressure it would take to break the skin on the back of my hand? Preston? The tennis pro and his killer serve?

"Am I late?" Daisy stood in the entrance to the card room wearing a camel-colored twin set and a smile.

"You're right on time." For once. Thank God.

Jinx pulled her hand away.

I slipped my hand into my lap and glanced down. Red crescents marred the skin.

"I saw Libba parking her car on my way in."

"Good. We can start on time for once." Every minute she'd spent waiting on Daisy (and there had been lots of them) had been wasted. That's what Jinx's tone conveyed.

Daisy's eyes filled with tears. Was she wounded by the unkindness of Jinx's words or their tone?

"We'll get to spend more time together." The brightness I forced into my voice sounded brittle. "Daisy, come sit down. Today is the day you can tease Libba about being the last one here."

Daisy sat and directed her doe-eyed gaze at Jinx. "Someone woke up on the wrong side of the bed this morning." Daisy had young children and was given to mothering inanities. *Don't cry over spilled milk. Sticks and stones may break my bones, but words will never hurt me. You can't judge a book by its cover.* All of them completely foolish, unless it was actual milk that was spilled and not something bigger. Like blood.

Libba breezed in, took the temperature of the room, and stuck her head back into the hallway. "Carlos, when you have a moment, we're going to need a bottle of wine. Put it on my account."

We played a rubber in near silence.

Libba ordered a second bottle of wine. It was the second bottle that loosened our tongues.

"How's Grace?" Daisy asked. "Finding another body at your house must be terribly upsetting for her."

"She seems to be handling it well."

"Still..." Daisy sounded doubtful.

"She said Grace was fine." Jinx's voice was a bit slurry. Apparently she'd had more than her fair share of the first bottle of wine.

Libba glanced at me and raised a single brow. *Did I know what was going on?*

I did. I shrugged as if I didn't.

"So tell us about this party tomorrow night, Ellison." At least Libba was trying to be pleasant.

"It's the benefactors' party for a luncheon my cousin Cora is chairing."

"Cora?" Daisy cocked her head to the side.

"She's married to Mother's first cousin Thornton."

Daisy shook her head. "I can't picture her."

"She's mousy." The left corner of Jinx's upper lip curled into a sneer. "She lets that husband of hers walk all over her."

I would have liked to argue (maybe not, given Jinx's mood), but I'd have lost the argument because Jinx was right.

"Now, Jinx," said Daisy. "We never really know what goes on in another woman's marriage."

My jaw dropped. Daisy shared mommy inanities, not pearls of wisdom.

Then she added, "Ellison's cousin could be perfectly happy."

The hinge on my jaw resumed normal function. There was the Pollyanna Daisy with whom I played bridge every week, her rose-colored glasses firmly positioned on the bridge of her nose. One need only glance at Cora to know she and Thornton did not enjoy a happy marriage.

We let Daisy's comment sit on the table. No one was willing to respond.

Daisy shifted in her chair and smiled brightly. "Who do you think killed Khaki?"

All things being equal, I'd rather talk about Cora. "No idea."

"I've been thinking." Daisy's mouth thinned and she rubbed her right hand across her eyes. See no evil.

"And?" asked Libba.

"Well—" Daisy caught her upper lip in her teeth and glanced around the card room, empty except for us. "Do you think your last decorator would...I mean...I heard she was furious."

"At me. Not Khaki." Even though I'd had just cause to let her go, Olivia Forde's cheeks paled and her mouth drew into a snarl when I told her someone else would be redecorating the study.

"I don't know, Ellison." Libba took a contemplative sip of wine. "Khaki had been getting jobs with lots of people that Olivia expected to get."

"Olivia?" I shook my head. Of all the possible motives, murder over clients seemed the most far-fetched.

"Then who?" insisted Daisy. "Who do you think killed her?"

I forced my gaze to Daisy. No sneaking a peek at Jinx...nope. Nope. Not doing it. Daisy wore her twin set and her pearls with aplomb. She actually looked pulled together and not like something the cat dragged in. She was who I needed to look at not...My head turned. Dammit. I dropped my gaze to my lap.

Some awful, disloyal, horrible part of me insisted on knowing how Jinx was reacting to this conversation.

I examined my cuticles instead. "I have no idea." If only I felt as sure as I sounded.

I drove home with rain spattering the windshield. The wipers' swish sounded more like *Was it Jinx?* than a swish. I ignored them.

Not.

"She didn't do it." Mine was the only voice in the car except for Harry Chapin's, and he was too busy singing about a man who neglected his family to listen to me.

I pulled into the drive (blessedly free of cars that weren't supposed to be there) and hurried inside. "I'm home," I called.

"We're in the kitchen." Grace sounded as if she might be getting a cold.

The kitchen was warm and welcoming and smelled like hot

chocolate. Aggie and Grace, their hands wrapped around mugs, were perched on stools at the island, and Max lay near a vent soaking up heat.

I dropped a kiss on the top of Grace's head. "How was school?"

"Fine."

"How was your math test?"

"Fine."

"Anything interesting happen today?" There was a question she couldn't answer with *fine*.

"Not really." She sounded nonchalant. Suspiciously nonchalant.

I poured myself a cup of hot chocolate and joined them at the island. "Nothing?"

"Dawn and Trip broke up."

Trip I knew. His grandmother played bridge with Mother. He'd beaten a piñata to smithereens at one of Grace's early birthday parties.

He preferred Batman to Superman.

"Do I know Dawn?"

"I doubt it." Three words. Three words that sounded so much like Mother they stole my breath. Three words. They conveyed all I ever needed to know. Dawn was not our kind. I never would know her. And Trip Michaels was better off without her. Grace had no business sounding like that.

I crossed my arms.

"There's no reason to look like that," she said.

"Like what?"

"Like you just sucked a lemon." Grace swung her ponytail. "All I meant was that she didn't grow up here."

"Mhmm." I had my doubts.

"Seriously, Mom, lighten up."

Just what every parent wanted to hear.

"Aunt Sis called. She wants you to phone her."

"Is everything all right?" My aunt was in Ohio with her son so that my sister could donate a kidney to him.

"She sounded fine. Call her. By five." Grace stood. "I have homework."

Aggie watched her go. "Teenagers should come with an instruction manual."

"That would take all the fun out of raising them."

"She's a good kid."

I didn't argue. Instead I nodded and sipped my cocoa.

"I cleaned the foyer after your mother left." Aggie's voice tiptoed through a mine field.

"What did she do?" Mother was fully capable of returning and critiquing Aggie's cleaning techniques.

"Nothing." The *but* in Aggies voice was wider than the fairway on the twelfth hole.

"What's wrong?"

She stood, opened a drawer, and withdrew a plastic sandwich bag.

Nestled inside was a matchbook. I'd seen a matchbook like that once before.

"Where did you find that?"

"With the umbrellas in the stand in the foyer."

The brass umbrella stand gleamed from regular polishing. There was no way the matchbook in Aggie's plastic bag could have been there long.

"I polish on Thursdays." Meaning the matchbook had appeared in the stand in the past week.

The seemingly innocent matchbook was anything but. At some point between Thursday and now, the matches had migrated from Lord-knew-where to my foyer. And it wasn't just any matchbook. It was black. The darkness lightened only by a name in silver metallic, Club K. It was only on closer inspection that one noticed the tiny pair of handcuffs. I didn't need to inspect more closely. My late husband had been a habitué of Club K. I was all too familiar with the matchbook and what happened at the club it advertised.

I closed my eyes, gripped the edge of the counter, and waited for the room to stop spinning. "I don't suppose..."

"It wasn't there last week."

Damn. How twisted was it that I'd hoped a matchbook from a sex club belonged to my husband?

"Someone came into the house, reached into their pocket, pulled something out, and this—" Aggie poked at the bag with the tip of her nail "—fell out."

Most likely the *something* was a gun. Most likely that gun was used to shoot Khaki. "We have to tell Anarchy."

"I know." She didn't sound remotely happy.

Condemned men on their way to the chair walked with more enthusiasm than I. Sure, the phone looked harmless enough, but the call I had to make would bring the police back to the house. What if they closed my foyer as a crime scene? What if they dusted for fingerprints in the rest of the house? What if they told us to leave entirely? Mother's party was a day away. She'd have apoplexy. And when she was done, there would be another murder. Mine.

I picked up the receiver. Slowly.

"You're certain you want to do that?" asked Aggie.

Not remotely.

I inserted my finger in the dial. "Murder is more important than a cocktail party."

"You're sure?"

Nope.

I dialed.

The call that brought Anarchy back to the house took three minutes.

Ten minutes elapsed before he arrived at my door.

Unfortunately, he did not come alone.

Detective Peters scowled at the umbrella stand as if it had conspired with a hat tree to hide evidence.

Anarchy scowled at Aggie and her sandwich baggie of evidence.

"I can't believe our people missed evidence," growled the rumpled detective.

Did Peters think we'd planted the matchbook?

He held out his hand for the baggie and Aggie gave it to him.

He lifted the matchbook to eye level and squinted. "Club K. You know this place, Jones?"

"Yeah."

I leaned against the wall. Almost wished I could slide down it.

"What's with the handcuffs?"

My lips remained firmly sealed. Anarchy could explain to his partner that the matches came from a sex club.

"Later." Anarchy returned his attention to Aggie. "Where exactly did you find the matches?"

"With the umbrellas."

"When was the last time the umbrellas were removed from the stand?" he asked.

"Last Thursday," said Aggie.

"You're sure these aren't yours?" Detective Peters shook the bag. His beady eyes narrowed and the corner of his mouth curled into a sneer.

"Positive. I don't smoke." And if I did, I wouldn't carry matches from Club K.

"Yours?" Peters directed his question to Aggie.

"No."

"Could they belong to your daughter?"

An appalled squeak escaped my lungs. "No!"

"Who has been here since Monday?" asked Peters.

"My mother and her staff. The matches do not belong to them."

"How can you be so sure?"

Mother didn't need whips or cuffs or nightmare-inducing apparatuses to bend people to her will. "They don't go to sex clubs."

If I hadn't been looking right at Detective Peters, I would have missed the lift of his eyebrows and the drop of his jaw. The expression lasted less than a second. He replaced shock with his customary you'd-better-respect-me-or-else scowl. "And you do?"

"Enough, Peters. I'll explain later." Anarchy looked intimidating without a scowl.

Peters looked from me to his partner then shrugged. "We need to get these dusted." He frowned at Aggie. "I suppose your prints are all over them?"

"Probably."

The unpleasant expression on Peters' face deepened and his fingers closed together as if he was imagining them closing on real handcuffs.

"The matches don't belong to anyone in this house," Aggie added.

"So your theory is that they belong to the killer?" Peters sounded snide.

"Who else?" I asked.

Anarchy directed his coffee-colored gaze at Aggie. "Did you find anything else?"

"No." She shook her head and her giant hoop earrings glinted in the late afternoon light.

Detective Peters grunted. "This is all too convenient." Did he think I'd planted evidence? Did he still consider me a suspect? "Don't either of you leave town."

He did.

# ELEVEN

Thursday passed in a whirl—the caterer, the liquor store, the florist, and the company that rented glasses all delivered their wares. The caterer claimed Aggie's kitchen. The bartender, Chester, arrived late in the afternoon and set up a full bar in the living room. The florist set a huge arrangement on my dining room table and smaller vases on every other surface.

By five o'clock, the house was perfect. Even the harpist was in place. Tucked into the farthest corner of the living room.

Good thing, too. At two minutes after five, Mother and Daddy arrived.

My father disappeared into the family room with a murmur about the evening news.

Mother was there to inspect. She moved through the public rooms of my home with an economy of effort that boggled the mind. Lord only knew the length of her internal checklist.

"Good evening, Chester." She could find no fault with the living room, the sunroom, or the smiling bartender. "Do you have plenty of limes and olives?"

"Yes, Mrs. Walford. I believe I do."

"May I have a martini please?"

"Dry?" he asked.

"Arid."

"Mother, what's wrong?" Daddy was the martini drinker, not Mother.

"The plane was delayed. The speaker can't join us this evening. This party has been a disaster from the word go." That might be true, but Mother's level of anxiety seemed higher than planes flew. And that was exceedingly unusual. Mother ate stress for breakfast. She didn't wear it in the corners of her mouth.

"I'm sure everyone will understand."

"They won't. But this is Cora's fault. She should have booked a flight for much earlier in the day." Mother accepted a drink from Chester and drank deeply. "I need to check the dining room."

I trailed after her.

Snowy white damask covered the length of the table and the floral arrangement—spider mums and bittersweet—was flanked by my great-grandmother's candlesticks. Tapers that mirrored the color of the bittersweet waited for a flame while sterling serving dishes waited for food.

"This looks lovely."

Praise? "Mother are you feeling all right?"

"Fine." She patted the perfect helmet of her hair. "Is Hunter coming tonight?"

There was a question I didn't care to answer. "Um…"

*Ding dong*

Saved by the bell.

Mother glanced at her watch. "That will be Thornton and Cora. I told her to arrive early to check on things." The unsaid *I shouldn't have to tell her that* hung in the air like a soap bubble.

"I'll get the door."

"Where's Aggie?" Mother's tone made it clear she thought my housekeeper should be answering the door, not helping me dodge questions.

"Supervising in the kitchen. I'm on door duty until the buffet goes out."

"You didn't change the menu, did you?"

"The caterer will pass rumaki."

She sniffed.

"I'd better get that door." I hurried into the front hall.

Cora stood on my front stoop. "Thornton will be a few minutes late." As greetings went it was weak.

"How lovely to see you." I beckoned her inside. "Please, come in."

A chill wind—one that smelled of impending snow—followed Cora into the foyer and snaked around my legs. I shivered. "It's cold out there."

She nodded. Barely. As if she hadn't noticed the biting cold.

One of the caterer's extra staff materialized. "May I take your coat, ma'am?"

Cora shrugged out of a grey cashmere coat, took off her gloves, jammed them in a pocket (they'd be wrinkled later), and handed over the coat.

"We're putting the coats in the blue room upstairs, ma'am." The young man turned and climbed the stairs.

Cora watched him go. She wore a pale beige sack. Well, maybe not a sack. Cora's dress wasn't that flattering. She pressed her palms against her hips, smoothed the fabric, and took another step into the foyer. "Thank you for doing this, Ellison. I know it's an imposition."

"Not at all." I scratched the end of my nose.

"It is. I know it is. Especially now that the speaker can't be here. And I'm grateful. Thornton so wants this luncheon to be a success."

"What do you want?" The question popped out, unexpected and fully formed like Athena springing from Zeus' head.

Cora's eyes widened, her brows rose, and her mouth formed a perfect circle. She blinked and the expression disappeared as quickly as it had come. In an instant. "I want what Thornton wants."

No she didn't. There was no way shy, retiring Cora wanted to be standing in my foyer waiting for fifty guests. She couldn't possibly enjoy planning luncheons (no one enjoyed that but Mother). And there was no way she liked having Mother boss her around.

"You can say no. A woman can always say no."

She snorted softly. "Maybe you can."

Mother bustled into the foyer looking like a general whose troops had appeared on a parade ground with their shirts untucked. "Cora, you're here." Her tone suggested Cora was late. "Where's Thornton?"

"He dropped me off. He'll be here in a few minutes."

Mother's expression turned indulgent, which is to say the thin line of her mouth softened. "Just like a man. Harrington's glued to the evening newscast." She directed her gaze at me. "What time is Hunter coming?"

"He's not." There was no way I was explaining why.

*Ding dong*

My gaze shifted to my wrist. Not yet a quarter after five. It had to be Thornton at the door. I gripped the handle and pulled, ready with a welcoming smile.

Aunt Sis, wrapped in a ruana, stood on the stoop. "Ellison, there you are. Do you realize how difficult it's been to get ahold of you?"

Difficult enough that I had no idea she was coming. Or staying. A small suitcase rested on the bricks next to her.

Behind me, Mother's sharp intake of breath, recognizable from a hundred yards away, expressed extreme displeasure. They'd been getting along so well. What was wrong?

"Is David all right?"

"He's fine."

I opened the door wider and a second chill gust assaulted my legs. "Come in out of the cold."

Aunt Sis picked up her suitcase, stepped inside, and looked around. "You're getting ready to entertain." No flies on Aunt Sis. "Frances, I didn't realize you'd be here." She dropped the case and wrapped Mother in a swirl of flowing fabric.

Mother's face, over Aunt Sis' shoulder, was slack. Shocked. And not in a what-a-fabulous-surprise-to-see-my-sister way. Mother looked—I narrowed my eyes and studied her carefully—worried.

Why?

The two sisters parted and Aunt Sis spotted Cora. If she was surprised by Cora's presence or her awful dress, my aunt hid it well. "How lovely to see you, Cora." She followed this pronouncement with another swirly hug.

If Mother had looked shocked, Cora looked petrified.

Aunt Sis, with her head hooked over Cora's stiff shoulder, didn't notice.

"Don't worry," Aunt Sis said. "I won't crash your party. I just need a place to lay my head tonight."

Manners, ingrained in me since birth, kicked in (Mother had only herself to blame). "Of course you must join the party, and I'm delighted you're here. Do you mind if I put you in the rose room? They're using the blue room for coats."

The young man from the caterer reappeared and hefted (Aunt Sis traveled with lead bricks masquerading as books) the small suitcase up the front stairs.

"The rose room is perfect." Aunt Sis eyed the floral arrangement resting on the bombe chest that sat in the foyer. "What's the occasion?"

"Cora is chairing a luncheon, and Ellison is hosting the benefactors' party." The way Mother said *benefactor* made it clear my aunt was not invited. Not unless she wanted to pull out her checkbook. Maybe not even then.

"Aunt Sis can attend as my guest."

"Thank you, Ellison." Aunt Sis's eyes positively twinkled. "But I'd like to lie down for a bit. Perhaps I'll join you later." She climbed the first few steps.

"Grace is upstairs in her room. She'd love to see you."

"And I'd love to see her."

Mother, Cora, and I watched Aunt Sis climb the rest of the stairs and disappear down a hallway.

"Oh my." Cora's words were nearly lost in a giant exhalation of breath.

"It's not a problem, Cora."

"What are you two talking about?" What was going on?

"Never you mind." Mother flipped her wrist, dismissing my question.

I did mind. A lot. "Now just a minute—"

*Ding dong.*

"Ellison, get the door." Mother was nothing if not imperious.

I stared at her for a few seconds—glowered, really—just so she knew I didn't appreciate being kept in the dark.

She ignored my glare. Mother was nothing if not impervious. To me. If Daddy had narrowed his eyes, lowered his brows and chin, and thinned his lips, Mother would have moved heaven and earth to remove the expression from his face. "Ellison, the door."

I swallowed a frustrated sigh and answered the door.

Thornton stood on the other side looking like a minor movie star. He had the strong jaw, the firm lips, the salt and pepper hair, and the physique. He'd have looked like a major movie star except for his eyes. I never liked my cousin's eyes. They had all the warmth of the arctic wind that entered with him.

He dropped the chilly whisper of a kiss on my cheek. "Ellison, you look lovely. Thank you so much for doing this."

"My pleasure."

"Frances, you look beautiful. That purple suits you."

He wasn't wrong. Mother, who wore a purple tweed Chanel suit which set off the brilliant white of her hair, looked positively regal. She lifted her hand, touched her pearls, and smiled up at him.

Thornton's gaze landed on Cora's beige sack and he shook his head as if she was a lost cause. "Frances picked out your dress for tomorrow, didn't she?"

Cora nodded. Poor woman. All she really needed was a belt and the right scarf tied at her neck.

Thornton shifted his gaze to the closed, locked door to Henry's study. "After the week you've had, I appreciate your opening your home."

As if I'd had a choice. "Happy to do it." The lie made my nose itch.

Thornton shifted his gaze back to Mother. "How many are we expecting tonight?"

"Around fifty. With the weather, a few people called to cancel. I encouraged my friends to send their children in their stead."

Thornton shrugged out of his coat and folded it over his arm.

"The young man who's helping with coats got detained upstairs." He'd probably herniated a disc lifting Aunt Sis' suitcase onto the rack.

"Cora can take it." He handed the coat to his wife.

Cora wasn't there to carry coats. "He'll be back in a moment."

Thornton waved away my words. "She doesn't mind, do you, dear?"

"Of course not." Cora's face looked pale and pinched. A trip up a staircase might finish her off.

I took the coat from Cora's hands. "Don't be silly. You're a guest in my home. Go get a drink. Chester's set up and ready in the living room. I'll run this upstairs."

No one moved.

"Go." I waved toward the living room. "Shoo."

They could suit themselves. I climbed the stairs, deposited Thornton's coat next to his wife's, headed to my bedroom and turned on the lights, pushing back the encroaching darkness.

There was something off tonight. Off beyond the unlikeliness of Mother and Cora sharing a secret. Off beyond Aunt Sis' sudden arrival and her decision to skip a party. The energy downstairs skipped and stuttered like a scratched LP. Something awful was going to happen. Certainty ran through my veins.

I opened my dresser drawer and withdrew a coiled crocodile belt. The shade of brown might not exactly match Cora's shoes, but it was close enough. Cora's frozen expression when she saw Aunt Sis flitted across my brain, and my fingers tightened around the belt. What was Aunt Sis up to? "You're being silly," I murmured. The Ellison in the mirror hanging above the dresser didn't believe me, Aunt Sis was always up to something.

"Silly." I opened a second drawer and my fingers closed on the heavy silk twill of an Hermes scarf. The muted colors would work with Cora's beige. "Nothing is going to happen tonight."

The Ellison in the mirror cocked her chin and shook her head.

I turned my back on her, went into the bathroom, and grabbed a tube of soft pink lipstick. Cora's thin lips could do with some color. Of course, Ellison in the mirror was there too. Stony-faced with certainty that disaster waited to pounce.

I turned off the light and headed downstairs to the living room where Mother and Thornton were deep in conversation and Cora stood alone, picking at the napkin on her cocktail glass. "Cora, would you come into the kitchen with me? Please?"

She paused, looked at Thornton as if waiting for permission.

He didn't bother looking at her. "If Ellison needs your help, go."

I led Cora to the kitchen. "I hope you won't be cross with me, but I thought that dress would look so much better with a belt. I grabbed one when I was upstairs." Before she could object, I looped the narrow belt around her waist.

She was truly slender, there was no explaining why she hid her figure in frumpy dresses.

"You do the buckle," I instructed.

With shaking fingers, she complied.

"Perfect. Now, how about a scarf? It will soften the neckline of your dress." I folded the scarf into a triangle, tied it around Cora's neck, and fluffed. "Lovely." I pulled out my final prop—the lipstick—and handed it to her. "It's a soft pink and very flattering."

I took putting on lipstick for granted, could do it with my eyes closed. Not Cora. She pressed hard enough to push her thin lips to the side, finished, and returned the tube to me.

"Smoosh your lips together. Like this." I demonstrated.

Cora smooshed.

I stood back and admired. She looked infinitely better. "Thornton won't recognize you."

She swallowed loud enough for me to hear the lump in her throat. "Thank you." Tears stood in her eyes. "You're very kind."

"My pleasure." I grabbed a stray cocktail off the kitchen counter and handed it to her.

She daubed her eyes.

"What's up with you and Mother?" I asked, my voice light as the meringue dotting the dessert tartlets laid out on silver trays.

Cora stiffened. "Nothing."

The certainty that we were barreling toward disaster took me by the throat and shook. "You're sure?"

Cora nodded. "Positive. I'd better go back. Thornton will be wondering where I am." She pushed through the kitchen door.

I watched her go. Cora was lying.

# TWELVE

I stood at the door, welcomed Cora's benefactors into my home, and wished I'd had the sense to throw a sweater over my shoulders. The first snowflakes charmed. The thousands that followed did not. It was too early in the season for such weather, but every time I opened the door a fresh gust of snow and cold assaulted me.

"Lorna, how lovely to see you." Lorna, one of Mother's friends, had her son in tow. I held out my hand to him. "Tom, what a treat."

Tom took my hand in his and shook.

"Is Laurie coming?"

"She's at home." Lorna answered for her son. "I didn't want to brave the roads alone."

"Of course not. This nice young man will take your coats upstairs."

They took off their coats and handed them over.

"You should have had valet parking, dear." Like Mother, Lorna didn't pull her punches.

Tom offered me an apologetic shrug. When your mother was a termagant there wasn't much else you could do. This I knew.

"You're absolutely right, Lorna. My only excuse is that there was no snow in the forecast."

"Hmph." She looked as if she had more to say. Lots more.

"Why don't you go into the living room and warm up? The fire is roaring, and Chester has a bar set up."

"An excellent idea." Was it the fire or the drink that trumped telling me how I'd failed? Or both?

With an apologetic glance my way, Tom escorted his mother into the living room.

*Ding dong.*

I steeled myself for another blast of cold and opened the door.

Daniel Fleming waited on the other side, his arm draped around a woman half his age. For a moment, reality rendered me mute. Reality was ex-wives living in efficiency apartments and spritzing perfume at makeup counters because they had no job skills. Reality was their ex-husbands reliving their youths with girls not yet old enough to know better. Reality was rather bleak.

"Daniel." I waved him and the girl into my home. "Welcome."

"Don't close that door!" Jinx and Preston hurried up the front steps.

I blinked, quite sure they weren't on the guest list. "Come in."

Jinx didn't tarry. She entered the foyer and stamped her feet a time or two (her pumps were not made for snow). "The weather is wretched so Mother stayed home. She insisted we come in her place."

Preston stepped forward and dropped a polite kiss on my cheek. "Thank you for letting us crash your party."

"Don't be silly, I'm delighted you're here."

"We'll just grab a quick drink, say hello to Cora, and be on our way," said Jinx. "The roads are getting slick."

"I don't blame you a bit. Here's the young man to take your coats." I really needed to ask for the young man's name.

Jinx and Preston de-coated, de-scarfed, and in Preston's case, de-galoshed.

"You know Daniel Fleming, don't you? And this is his friend..."

"Cherry," he supplied. Oh dear Lord—if Mother met her I'd be treated to a treatise on why people should not name their children after food.

Preston shook Daniel's hand.

Jinx managed a polite smile. "How nice to meet you, Cherry." She turned to me. "We'll get out of your hair." Now she addressed the group. "Let's go find a drink."

*Ding dong.*

I shivered in advance of opening the door.

Mary Beth and Pete Brewer stood on the other side.

That was a surprise. Last I'd seen them Mary Beth was having dinner with a divorce attorney.

I forced a smile. "I'm so glad you could come. Come inside and get out of the cold."

They took my suggestion and I closed the door behind them.

"What a treat to have you here," I said.

"We wouldn't have missed it," said Pete.

Really?

"I'm a fan," he added.

I ought to ask about the speaker. Probably I should have asked already. Except I didn't much care who was speaking. I'd donated my table to the event; it wasn't as if I was going to hear their talk.

Mary Beth wore a pained smile. "How's your housekeeper?"

"Aggie?" Mary Beth had been in the parking lot when Bess died. "She's fine."

"She seemed genuinely upset."

"She was. Her husband gave her that car years ago."

"And she drove it until it fell apart?" Pete stepped behind Mary Beth and helped her shrug out of her coat.

"She did." Rattles and knocks and rust and all.

The young man from the catering company descended the stairs.

"Oh good, here's..."

"Roberto," he supplied.

"Roberto. He's here to take your coats."

Pete gave Roberto Mary Beth's coat then shrugged out of his own.

"Everyone is in the living room." I waved toward the room that held liquor, a fire, and even a harpist. "Please, go make yourselves at home."

Mary Beth paused, her gaze landing on the only closed door in the foyer. "Is that where..."

Where Khaki had died? "Yes." Dread. That was the word that described the sick feeling in my stomach. Dread.

"It seems so awful. We were in the parking lot of the Milgrim's and someone was in your house killing her."

I nodded. Awful didn't begin to cover it.

"Khaki was working for us too. Did you know?"

"No. I didn't realize." Apparently Khaki had kept very busy.

"Ridiculously expensive." Pete draped an arm across Mary Beth's shoulders. "Let's get you out of this cold." He jerked his chin toward the living room filled with warmth and liquor and people.

Mary Beth glanced up at him, her face pale with the memory of her dead decorator. "Of course, dear." But she lingered. Lingered and leaned. "You saw us at our worst," she whispered. She meant the restaurant where Pete had made such a scene. "I decided to give him one more chance."

"You know best." Cheaters cheated. Almost as if they couldn't help themselves. I had firsthand knowledge.

She offered me a small, tight smile and followed her husband into the living room.

People arrived in groups after that. Fours and sixes. Air kisses and cold ankles and polite platitudes. Everyone hurried to the living room. At six o'clock I left my post at the front door and checked the dining room.

Mother had selected shrimp curry and steamed rice served with pineapple and date chutney. There were poppadoms. There were gingered coconut chips. There were cold poached eggs settled onto artichoke bottoms held together with aspic. The food sat on polished silver. Someone had lit the tapers. Everything was perfect.

I popped into the kitchen. "Aggie, I've given up front door duty. I'll tell everyone they can help themselves to the buffet."

She nodded. "I'll listen for the doorbell."

The living room was filled with genteel chatter and soft strums from the harp in the corner. From the entrance, I said, "The buffet is open."

A few heads swiveled my way.

My heels sank into the soft carpet when I stepped inside. The group closest to me included Jinx, Preston, Mary Beth, and Pete.

"Please, be brave." I pressed my hands together as if in prayer. "Start the buffet line."

Jinx's gaze slid toward Mother. "Curry?"

"Of course."

Jinx glanced at the window that reflected sleek cocktailers and not the snow outside.

"We'll get the ball rolling," said Pete. He was a big man. Hopefully he wouldn't decimate the curry all by himself.

"Thank you," I said.

"My pleasure." He took Mary Beth's elbow and guided her toward the door.

The benefactors filtered out after Pete and Mary Beth.

"Go remind people there are other places they can sit." Mother stood beside me. "There aren't enough seats in here."

I nodded and headed to the dining room. "If you'd like, you're welcome to eat in the family room. It's just across the hall."

A few couples carried their plates that direction.

Jinx and Preston entered the dining room. "We decided to stay." Jinx lifted a plate. "We'll save you a seat in the living room."

Then came the flood, the dining room table hidden behind a wave of hungry people.

Finally, only Mother and Daddy, Cora and Thornton, and I remained. "Please." I gestured toward the buffet. "Help yourselves."

Thornton picked up a plate and filled it. "This looks delicious. All my favorites."

Really? Curry was one of those things I'd eat if it was served to me, but not a dish I'd ever pick.

Daddy tilted his chin toward the table. "Cora, Frances, help yourselves." He smiled at me. "You too, Ellison."

I shook my head. "My house. I go last."

He pursed his lips but took a plate and followed Mother around the buffet.

I spooned a small amount of rice onto my plate and topped it with a smaller amount of curry. The cold poached eggs I skipped entirely. That Mother thought I would approve of this menu...

I carried my plate into the living room and claimed the seat Jinx had saved for me.

There was energy between couples. The charged connection of new love, the comfortable buzz of people who've been together since forever and still like each other, the caustic spark of those who are unhappy, and the tired flicker of those who've grown weary of each other's company. The energy between Jinx and Preston was as taut as barbed wire and twice as sharp.

Jinx lifted a fork to her mouth. "Preston loves curry."

Preston reached for his drink. "So do you, dear."

Ugh. They were not talking about curry.

Mary Beth and Pete, who sat at the other end of the couch, shifted uncomfortably.

I put my plate on the coffee table. "I need to check on things in the kitchen. Will you please excuse me a moment?"

Preston half-rose from his chair.

I held out my hand and stood. "Don't get up."

He sank back into the wingback.

I made my way toward the door to the hallway. Smiling. Nodding. Asking if so-and-so was getting enough to eat, and promising a different so-and-so that the staff would be in soon to take their plate and serve dessert and coffee.

Thornton grabbed my arm and stopped me. "It's a nice party, Ellison. Thank you." He glanced around the full living room. "Cora could never have pulled this off."

"Of course she could."

He scowled. Because he disliked me disagreeing with him or because he thought his wife couldn't host a party for fifty?

"Thornton, I really need to—"

*Ding dong*

If I walked into the front hall, I'd have to answer the door, and I couldn't face another gust of cold air. I tarried. "I really need to tell you how pleased I am that I could help out."

His face smoothed. "Hopefully the luncheon will be as successful as tonight."

"I'm just sorry the weather didn't cooperate."

That brought a furrow back to his brow. "Have you heard a forecast?"

"No. I didn't realize it was supposed to snow tonight."

"It wasn't. The weatherman said this would go north." His tone suggested he held the weatherman personally responsible.

Aggie, who wore an understated black kaftan, slipped into the living room and walked toward me. "Mr. White is here." Her voice was low.

Mother, who sensed problems like other people sensed rain on their skin or sunshine in their eyes, appeared next to us. "Stan White? What's he doing here?" Her voice carried surprise and volume. She adjusted the volume to a much lower decibel. "Any idiot can see you're entertaining."

"Mr. White would like a word with Mrs. Russell."

"Now? Absolutely not." Mother lowered her voice to a furious whisper. "You can't keep embroiling yourself in murders."

"Mother—" I attempted a soothing tone "—it's all right. It'll only take a minute."

"It most certainly is not *all right*. You have guests you haven't even spoken to yet."

Mother wasn't wrong. I looked around the full living room. I'd stopped by to chat with everyone, but I still needed to make the rounds in the family room.

"Aggie, please see if Mr. White would like some dinner. Last I checked there was plenty of curry left." Of course there was. It was curry. "I'll see him as soon as I'm able."

Aggie nodded, a grim expression on her face.

A sick feeling tightened my stomach. What did Stan want? "Maybe I should just—"

"Have you made the rounds in the family room?" Mother's question was rhetorical. She knew the answer.

"I'll do it now." Complying was easier and probably faster than arguing.

I made my way to the family room where Lorna caught me

with one swipe of her turkey vulture hands. "Lovely party, Ellison. I adore curry." She meant it.

I glanced at Tom's plate—a study in pushing food around without eating a bite. Obviously he didn't adore curry.

"Someone will be by with dessert and coffee." No one disliked lemon meringue tartlets. And if they did, we also had pumpkin tartlets topped with dollops of whipped cream.

I smiled at Ellen Byron who was entertaining a group with stories about her Louisiana relatives. I winked at Jack Kelly who crouched next to octogenarian Bernice Danner. I traded air kiss with Susan Archer. And when I'd interacted with every single person in the room, I headed to the dining room to see Stan.

Someone had put out the candles. Without their flames reflecting in the windows, the room transformed from cozy to eerie. I squinted at the table. Not only was the candle out, but the candlestick was missing. I reached for the rheostat and turned up the chandelier.

I wasn't mistaken. The candlestick was gone.

Mother would have kittens.

"Stan?" My voice shook. Dammit. I stepped farther into the room and steadied my voice. "Stan?"

Being afraid was just silly. Sixty people were wandering around my house. It wasn't as if I was alone. But I was alone in the dining room. All alone. With my heart lodged somewhere near the back of my throat.

The sick feeling in my stomach—the one that had plagued me all night—moved to a variety of other intestines.

The voices of the catering crew in the kitchen were clearly audible. I was fine.

I took another step into my dining room. Normal except for the missing candlestick and the—

And the foot extending beyond the edge of the table.

Oh dear Lord.

"Stan?"

Another step.

And another.

Stan lay on the floor, his body stretched out as if he were napping.

He wasn't.

My great-grandmother's candlestick lay next to him—it's silver shine colored red. And there was *matter* on the heavy end.

Sweet nine-pound baby Jesus.

My stomach flipped. My heart tried to escape my chest. I stumbled backward. "Aggie!"

# THIRTEEN

Mr. White in the dining room with a candlestick.

My life was turning into a sinister board game.

Aggie stood next to me. Gaping. "Is he...?"

"I think so." Nausea welled up from my stomach. I covered my mouth with my hand and jerked my head toward the kitchen.

Together we escaped the carnage in the dining room, stopping only to turn out the lights. Hopefully the people populating the first floor would think the buffet was closed. Hopefully no one would stumble over Stan's body.

"Get Mrs. Russell a glass of water," Aggie directed one of the caterer's staff.

I sank onto a stool. Accepted the glass. Sipped. I stared at my lap, studying the subtle pattern of my dress until the urge to vomit ebbed. I raised my head. "We need to call."

"On it." Aggie, whose brow was as wrinkled as a Shar-Pei's, picked up the phone and dialed.

"Ellison, are you in here?" Mother pushed through the swinging door. "Do you realize someone has turned out the lights in the dining room?" She stopped, narrowed her eyes, and somehow drew herself up so that she was taller than her actual height. "What's happened?"

"Someone murdered Stan White." My voice was flat. Apparently I'd left all my emotion in the dining room.

The color leeched out of Mother's cheeks and she staggered.

"Aggie is calling Anarchy now. Do you want a glass of water?"

"Good Lord, no." Mother pointed to a young woman wearing a chef's coat. "You. Go get me a brandy. Now."

Fortunately, the woman was smart enough not to argue.

Mother claimed a stool at the island. "This is a disaster."

"Especially for Stan."

"Don't be smart, Ellison." She put her elbows on the counter and rested her head in her hands. "He was shot?"

"No." I drained my glass. Too bad I hadn't asked for brandy like Mother. "His skull was bashed in."

Mother's already pale cheeks turned the color of parchment. "With what?"

Someone took the empty glass from my hand, refilled it, and returned it to me. I sipped. Slowly.

Next to me Mother sighed. I knew that sigh. It spoke of a daughter who was a disappointment. A major disappointment. Just wait. When I told her how Stan was murdered, her head was going to levitate off her body and spin, spewing fire and destruction upon us all. An experience that *required* brandy. "Great-grandmother's candlestick." I spoke fast and low and ran the syllables together.

Mother didn't react. Didn't move. But I know she heard me because I heard her. "Fudge."

"I have Detective Jones on the line," said Aggie. "Do you want to speak with him?"

I stood, somehow made it across a few feet of kitchen floor, and took the phone from her hand.

"Anarchy, there's been another murder."

Anarchy did not say "fudge." No soft-selling expletives for him. He used the real word. Five times in a row. Then apologized for cursing.

"Stan White is in my dining room."

"And you're sure he's dead?"

"Pretty sure." My voice was dry as old bones. I closed my eyes and saw Stan's bashed head against the back of my lids. Ugh. I opened my eyes and stared at the desserts still sitting on the kitchen island.

The woman in the chef's coat returned with Mother's drink. I pointed at myself then the glass and mouthed the word, "Please."

She turned on her heel and went out the way she'd entered.

"What was Stan White doing at your house?" asked Anarchy.

"He came by to talk to me."

I could imagine Anarchy's forehead buried in the expanse of his palm. "What did he say?"

"Nothing. I didn't get a chance to speak with him."

"Why not?" Frustration was creeping into Anarchy's voice.

"I'm hosting a party."

This pronouncement was met with a few seconds of silence. Seconds that lasted an eternity. "How many people?"

"Umm..." I looked at Mother. "How many people showed up?"

"Forty-two." She looked a smidge happier now that she had a drink. Where was mine?

"Forty-two," I repeated. "Plus the catering staff. And the harpist."

"The harpist?"

"Don't ask. Also, Aunt Sis is here. All told, there are at least fifty people in the house."

"Don't let anyone leave. I'm on my way." He hung up.

"Well?" Mother pinched the bridge of her nose.

"No one can leave."

She swore again. Except this time, she didn't say "fudge."

The woman returned with my drink. I took a sip, enjoyed the burn in my throat, and waited for the inevitable from Mother.

"How many times have I told you that this must stop?" It was a rhetorical question.

I answered anyway. "At least a hundred. Maybe more."

"Yet you continue to find bodies." Mother put her glass down on the counter so hard the brandy sloshed over the rim.

"It's not as if I find them on purpose."

"Can't you just pretend you don't see them?"

"Someone is going to notice a body in the dining room. And, if we ignore it, it will start to smell."

"Don't be smart with me, young lady."

The catering staff was watching us as if we were engaged in a particularly grueling volley in a tennis match. Their heads swiveled with each comment.

"It's pretty easy to be smart when you say such inane things."

"I am trying to help."

"By lecturing me? I don't enjoy finding bodies, Mother. It's extremely unsettling." My stomach flipped at the reminder of just how unsettling the sight of Stan's bashed head was. I sent my long-suffering stomach some brandy. "Helping would be managing the guests. Someone is going to want to leave soon and they can't."

Mother turned her gaze to the woman in the chef's coat. "Is your staff passing desserts and coffee?"

"Of course," she squeaked.

Not all of them were. Two were watching us with a level of attention usually reserved for a new episode of *All in the Family*.

"Get out there," Mother snarled.

The staff, revealing heretofore unsuspected sense, grabbed trays of desserts and disappeared through the swinging doors.

Mother turned her incensed gaze on Aggie. "You. Go to the front door and head off anyone who wants to leave." Mother pointed a finger at me. "You. You stay here. If your guests can't find you to thank you, they'll have to stay."

I wasn't so sure about that. There'd been plenty of times I'd tried to find my hostess, failed, and left without expressing my thanks. I soothed my guilty conscience by sending flowers the next day.

Mother picked up her glass and drained the rest of her brandy. "I'll go manage this disaster."

Her meaning was clear. She'd clean up my mess, but she'd hold it against me for years.

At least she was actually helping.

I was left alone with the woman in the chef's coat who busied herself with filling another silver tray with tartlets. "Your mother has a strong personality," she said.

Attila the Hun had a strong personality. Mother was a mile-wide tornado with hundred-fifty-mile-per-hour winds.

The caterer wedged a pecan tartlet onto the already full tray. "I don't think I'd be able to stand up to her the way you do."

Me? Stand up to Mother?

I had.

The glow in my stomach had nothing—almost nothing—to do with the brandy.

The police arrived. Squad cars with men in uniform. Detective Peters with his disreputable raincoat. And Anarchy.

They interviewed the guests.

And me.

Presumably they asked us the same questions—although I'd bet I was the only one lucky enough to face the cantankerous Detective Peters. He regarded me with suspicious eyes and a slight sneer. "Where were you between seven thirty and eight fifteen?"

I glanced around the study, opened as an interrogation room. Was it just four days ago I'd found Khaki on the carpet? Those four days felt like an eternity. "I floated between the living room and family room."

"Floated?"

"Floated. I visited with guests, made sure they were getting plenty to eat, had their drinks refilled." Did he not understand what a hostess did?

"In all that floating—" he made it sounded as if I'd been doing something dirty "—did you notice anyone acting strangely?"

"No."

"Did you float into the dining room?"

"No."

He grunted and made a note on the small pad he pulled out of the pocket of his raincoat. "Did you know Stan White?"

"To say hello to."

"Who would want to kill him?"

"I have no idea."

The curl of Detective Peters' lip became more pronounced. "Yet he's dead in your dining room and someone in this house killed him."

I wasn't about to argue the dead part of his statement, but I held out hope for person or persons unknown. "How can you be so sure it was someone in the house? Maybe an intruder snuck in and bashed him over the head."

Detective Peters leaned back in his chair and crossed his arms. A smile flitted across his face. There were people who delighted in sharing bad news. It was like manna to them. Detective Peters was obviously one of those people.

Oh dear.

"Jones walked around your house when he got here." Peters looked out the window where the snow had tapered off but still fell. "There were no tracks leading away from this place. Either the killer is one of your guests or you have an intruder hiding in your home."

The man was pure joy and light.

He glanced at his little notepad. "What made you go into the dining room?"

"Someone had turned the lights off."

"Why didn't you just turn them on and leave?"

"I did turn them on, but I noticed a candlestick was missing from the table. I stepped inside to look for it and found Stan."

"And the candlestick."

"And the candlestick." Covered with blood and—I shuddered—*matter.*

"You'll need to vacate the premises."

Again? Now I looked out the window. He wanted us to leave in a snow storm? "No." I'd stood up to Mother. Standing up to Detective Peters ought to be easy.

His irascible glare burned into me. "It's not a request."

I spread my damp palms across my knees and steeled my spine. "Detective Peters, my father plays golf with the police commissioner. All it takes is one phone call and I stay here."

Somehow his glare became more choleric.

I smiled sweetly and gripped my knees to hide the shaking of my hands.

"Need I remind you that an intruder may be hiding in your home?"

I increased the sweetness of my smile. "I'm sure your men are searching thoroughly."

He mumbled something. *Uppity bit?* No. *Uppity bitch.*

"We're not leaving." I used my hostess voice. It said welcome, I'm so glad you're here, and was almost impossible to argue with.

"Peters, one of the uniforms has got something." Anarchy spoke from the doorway.

Detective Peters grunted, gave me a this-isn't-over scowl, and stood. "She says she doesn't know anything."

*She* was in the room. *She* didn't like being spoken about as if *she* wasn't there. Her sweet smile slipped.

Anarchy's coffee-colored gaze bounced between his partner and me. "Why don't I finish this up?"

Detective Peters grunted. Again. The man was positively Neolithic.

Was this part of their plan? Bad cop, good cop? If so, the plan was destined for failure. I didn't know anything.

Anarchy claimed Peters' empty chair across from me, and Peters, thank heavens, left.

"How are you holding up?"

"I've had better nights."

"You've had worse ones too."

I couldn't argue that. "I'll be fine. Does your partner really think I killed Stan?"

"I doubt it."

"Why?"

"Because you'd have to stand on a chair to bash someone over the head. Someone with some height killed Stan White."

"Stan wasn't all that tall."

"At least five inches taller than you."

"If he doesn't think I'm a suspect, why is he so unpleasant?"

Anarchy's lips thinned to a tight line. "He's unpleasant to everyone. Plus, you keep finding bodies."

"Believe me, I wish I didn't."

He leaned forward and took my hands in his. "I do believe you. I also believe you frequently know more than you think you do."

My thoughts flew to Jinx and Preston. Preston was definitely taller than Stan. But why would Preston want Stan dead? I shook my head. "Not this time."

His grip on my hands tightened. "Are you sure? Two people have been murdered in your home."

"Are you going to move into the guest house again?" I asked. Anarchy had stayed in the suite in the carriage house when it seemed I was being targeted by a killer.

"Do you want me to?"

The air around us sparked. With a few words we'd set a pile of waiting tinder ablaze. My mouth went dry. My stomach quivered. I'd told Hunter not two days ago I wasn't ready for a relationship, and here I was...melting.

"I..."

He leaned closer and I smelled soap and snow and a scent unique to Anarchy.

"I..."

He let go of my hands and touched my cheek.

I'd told Hunter I wasn't ready. Why couldn't I tell Anarchy? Standing up to Mother. Standing up to Detective Peters. Standing on my own. That's what I wanted. Except, with the pad of Anarchy's finger running the length of my cheek, I wasn't so sure. My lips parted and I leaned toward him.

Our mouths touched and the spark in the air burned through me, firing nerve endings, firing *want*.

"Ellison, are you in here?" Mother barged through the door.

I jumped away from Anarchy's kiss as if I'd been scalded. Heat rose to my cheeks, and I held my suddenly frigid fingers against my face to cool the flush.

Anarchy was no help. He looked as guilty as I felt. If only he'd stop fiddling with his tie.

"What, Mother?"

Her narrowed gaze told me I wasn't fooling anyone, least of all her. "Your guests would like to leave."

I stood, smoothed my skirt, and somehow produced a shaky smile. "Coming."

"Go ahead." She waved me toward the front hall. "I'll join you in a moment. First I'd like a word with Detective Jones."

What did it say about me that I was glad to escape her?

And what did it say that the entire time I was shaking hands with people eager to depart, the entire time I was apologizing for the horrible inconvenience of a corpse in the dining room, I was wondering what Mother was saying to Anarchy?

# FOURTEEN

I waited for Mr. Coffee to work his magic, cup at the ready. The night had stretched into the wee hours and only caffeine could keep me going.

At least I had the kitchen to myself. Alone, I could ponder the significance of the almost-kiss.

I replayed every second, wanting to relive the moment Anarchy's lips met mine.

Instead, my brain caught on the lie I'd told. Anarchy had believed me when I told him I didn't know anything. My first instinct had been to protect my friends, but should I have told him about Jinx and Preston? With the morning sun reflecting off the snow, the light was too bright to ignore. Jinx and Preston were keeping secrets. From each other. From me.

What else did I know that I didn't know I knew? Maybe there was another suspect, one I didn't count among my dearest friends.

Karen Fleming?

Except Karen Fleming wasn't tall. Worse, she hadn't even been at my house last night. She couldn't be the killer. Still, something she'd said niggled at me.

"Is the coffee ready?" Grace burst into the kitchen wearing a huge smile.

Mr. Coffee gurgled.

"Let me get you a cup, Mom." She took the empty mug from my hand, filled it, and topped it with cream.

"Thank you." I accepted the ambrosia she offered. "You're awfully cheery this morning."

She took a cup from the cabinet. "Am I?"

Suspiciously so. None of us had gotten much sleep, and Grace wasn't at her happiest in the morning under the best of circumstances.

"I guess I'm happy to see Aunt Sis."

"Is she up?"

Grace nodded. "Yep. She'll be down in a minute."

"I told Aggie to come in late. We're on our own for breakfast. I could make eggs."

"No." Grace spoke with insulting alacrity. One fire on the stove (okay, three fires on the stove) and people think you can't fry eggs. "Cereal is fine."

"Maybe your aunt would like eggs."

"Just a piece of fruit." Aunt Sis spoke from the bottom of the back stairs. She sidled into the kitchen and went directly to Mr. Coffee. "You lead an exciting life, dear." She poured coffee into a cup and waved away the offer of cream. "Tell me, how did your mother convince you to host the party for that awful woman?"

Awful woman? "Cora? Why don't you like Cora?" It was like disliking kittens. "Mother's ceiling fell in. She couldn't host a party."

"No, not Co—"

"Aunt Sis, if you're going to borrow my car, we'd better head out. That's all right, isn't it, Mom? Aunt Sis needs a car today."

"Of course. What do you have against Cora?"

Grace put her mug down on the counter. "Gotta go, Mom. Love you. See you later."

The two hurried out the back door. "Coat?" I called.

Grace raced back into the house, grabbed her coat from the hook, and snagged one of mine. "For Aunt Sis."

"Fine."

She disappeared out the back door a second time.

I took another sip of coffee and stared into space. It was odd that neither my daughter nor my aunt had mentioned the murder. What were they up to?

Lord only knew.

I completed homey tasks. I fed Max. I loaded the dishwasher with the dirty mugs. I made a second pot of coffee. While it brewed I climbed the stairs to my bedroom and took a quick shower.

I wanted to think about Anarchy's lips.

What had Mother said to him?

I wanted to think about his touch on my cheek.

Should I have told him about Jinx and Preston?

I wanted to think about the sparks.

What was it that Karen Fleming had said? Whatever it was, it bothered me enough to deaden the sparks.

I towel dried my hair, threw on jeans and a sweater, and went downstairs for fresh coffee. The Junior League directory was in the desk in the family room. I dug the book out of the bottom drawer and dialed Karen's number.

She answered on the third ring. "Hello."

"Karen, this is Ellison Russell calling."

"Ellison." My name, nothing more.

"The other day when we were talking—"

"I'm so sorry about that. You must think I'm a complete lunatic."

"Not at all." Maybe a little. "Listen, you said something about Khaki and—"

*Beeeeeep.*

I held the receiver away from my ear. "Karen?"

"This is the operator. I have an emergency breakthrough for Ellison Russell from Libba Price."

I glanced at my watch. It wasn't yet nine. What was Libba doing up, much less having an emergency? "Karen, may I call you back?"

"Of course. Take the call. It's an emergency." Was that relief I heard in Karen's voice? The click of her receiver meeting the cradle echoed through the line.

If Libba's emergency was whether to wear navy or charcoal gray, I'd kill her.

"I'll connect you now, Mrs. Russell," said the operator.

A series of clicks followed, then I heard Libba. "Ellison, are you there?"

"What's wrong?" I demanded.

"It's Jinx. Can you come over?" Libba's voice was pitched high. Higher than I'd ever heard.

"Of course. What about Jinx?" The coffee in my stomach made an uncomfortable swirl.

"Just come. She's raving about Khaki and Preston and how Preston is going to be next. I think she's on something. Please come."

"I'm on my way."

"Thank you." She hung up the phone.

I grabbed my purse, jumped into the car and raced to the Plaza. Libba lived on the top floor of a high-rise that overlooked the shopping district. The view was fabulous. Not that I stopped to enjoy it. Not when Jinx was splayed bonelessly across Libba's couch.

"What did she take?" I picked up Jinx's wrist and felt for a pulse. It was there. Weak, but there.

"Valium? I don't know."

"Did she say anything before she passed out?"

"Only that Khaki and Preston were up to something and that it got Khaki killed. Maybe Stan too."

I'd worry about the murders later. "Have you called Preston?"

"No one is answering at their home and his office says he's out."

"Have you called an ambulance?"

"Do you think we need to?"

I stared at her. Dumbfounded. Jinx was practically comatose. "Yes. We need to."

"It's just that if emergency personnel come up here, half the town will know about this before we even get Jinx to the hospital."

I'd forgotten about Libba's nosy neighbor, Agnes Crane. "Fine. We'll take her to the ER." It had been weeks since I made a trip to the hospital emergency room. The staff probably missed me. "Can you help me get her to your car?"

Together we hefted Jinx off the couch and half-walked, half-dragged her to the elevator. Her head lolled forward and her ankles bent. If Agnes Crane stepped out of her apartment and saw us, there would be plenty of talk.

We were lucky. The elevator arrived before Agnes caught the scent of fresh gossip.

Libba pushed. I pulled. And somehow we got Jinx stretched out in the backseat of Libba's car.

Thankfully, it was a short drive to the hospital. When we arrived, I hopped out of the passenger's seat and hurried inside.

The woman at the admitting desk looked up from her paperwork and gave me a tight smile. "Hello, Mrs. Russell. How are you today?"

I knew they'd missed me.

"I have a friend. She's in the car. She's taken something."

Maybe it was the tone of my voice or the pallor of my skin, but the admitting nurse picked up a phone and had two men with a stretcher standing next to me in seconds.

"She's right outside." I led them to Libba's car and they gently extracted an unconscious Jinx from the backseat and wheeled her inside.

"Stay with her," said Libba. "I'll park and be inside in a minute."

I nodded and followed the gurney.

Of course they wouldn't let me into the actual emergency room. I wasn't family. I plopped into a cold hard plastic chair and waited. Someone would come, if only to ask what Jinx had taken.

A few minutes later, Libba joined me. "Any news?"

"Too soon," I replied. "Did Jinx say anything else before she passed out?" What had Libba reported? *Khaki and Preston were up to something and it got Khaki killed. Stan too.*

"Something about a phoenix. Maybe she was talking about Phoenix. I didn't understand."

Neither did I. "Do you want coffee?"

"Please."

"You wait here in case the doctor comes out. I'll run down to the coffee shop."

Libba nodded and shifted in her uncomfortable seat. "When you get back I want to try calling Preston again."

"Good idea."

I could find the hospital coffee shop blindfolded. I'd spent that much time there of late. I ordered two coffees and retraced my steps to Libba, who was pacing the waiting room.

"No one has been out yet." Her voice was thick. With worry or tears?

I handed her a cup of comfort. "I'll go ask."

I approached the admitting nurse. "Is there any news about my friend?"

"Not yet, Mrs. Russell. Someone will be out soon." Soon in hospital time could be five minutes or five hours.

I sighed. "Thank you."

Libba called Preston again. Reached no one again. Together we drank our coffee, took turns pacing, and stared at the nurse behind the desk as if our gazes could make someone appear with news.

I drained the last of my coffee, stood, and threw my empty cup in the trash. "I'm going to the powder room. I'll be back in a few minutes."

Libba merely nodded. It was her turn to pace and I'd disrupted the count of her steps.

The ladies' room smelled of rubbing alcohol and pine. I wrinkled my nose and stepped into a stall. Someone had taped a sign on the back of the door. The sign read, "Does he hurt you?" Beneath the question was a picture of a woman with a black eye. Beneath the picture was more text. "Call Phoenix House for help." A phone number followed.

I didn't read the phone number. I ignored the insistent urgings of my bladder. I ran back to the waiting area. "Libba!"

She'd returned to her seat and was flipping through a six-month-old copy of *Readers' Digest*.

"What?" She dropped the magazine onto her lap and it slid, unheeded, to the floor.

"Jinx said something about Phoenix?"

She nodded.

"What's the name of the charity board that Khaki sat on?"

"Phoenix House."

We let that settle into our brains.

"Preston is on the board," she added. "It's a shelter for abused women."

Maybe some angry husband was targeting board members? But if that were true..."Was Stan on the board?"

"No."

Both Khaki and Stan were dead. It couldn't be because of Phoenix House. Could it? "Did Jinx say why she thought Preston would be next?"

"She was almost incoherent. I have no idea."

Phoenix House. This whole mess had something to do with Phoenix House. I was sure of it. "I need some air. I'll be back in a few minutes." I stepped outside and was greeted by leaden skies and a cold wind. Another front had moved in. I scowled up at the ominous clouds. They matched my mood.

Phoenix House. Help for abused women. The only people who wouldn't support such an idea were abusers.

I crossed my arms over my chest and paced the sidewalk.

Had Khaki gotten crossways with an angry husband? What did Jinx know? Where was Preston?

The last question was answered with a screech of braking wheels. Preston George leapt from his car and raced through the emergency room doors without even seeing me.

I followed him inside, glad of the sudden burst of warmth.

Preston was leaning over the admitting desk and making demands.

Admitting nurses hated that. I knew firsthand.

I hurried to his side and rested my hand on his arm. "Preston."

"Ellison." He turned my name into a sob. "You brought her in?"

"With Libba."

Libba heard her name, put down whatever fascinating article she was reading in *Tiger Beat* (both David Cassidy and Donny Osmond were on the cover), and hurried over to us.

"Thank you." His voice caught. "So much."

"You're welcome." I patted his arm.

"We had a fight this morning and—"

I held up a finger, silencing him. "Is there any news about Mrs. George?" I asked the nurse.

"Soon." How many times could she say that with a straight face?

I led Preston away from her—to the far reaches of the waiting room. The nurse couldn't repeat what she couldn't hear.

Libba followed us. "You had a fight this morning and...?"

"Jinx is convinced that Khaki's murder has something to do with Phoenix House."

"You disagree?" I asked.

He nodded. "I do." He collapsed into one of the uncomfortable chairs. His head sank into his hands. "Unless—"

"Unless what?" Libba asked my question for me.

Preston lifted his head. "Have the doctors been out? Have you heard anything? Anything at all?"

Unless what? "Preston, please tell me—"

"Mr. George?" A man in a doctor's coat stood in front of us.

Preston shot out of his seat. "How is she?"

"We pumped her stomach."

"And?" Preston sounded desperate. Husband-who-still-loved-his-wife desperate.

"And she'll be fine."

"Thank God." Libba and I spoke in unison.

Preston swiped at his eyes, dashing away the tears that had appeared in the corner of his lids.

"You can see her," said the doctor.

All three of us stepped forward.

"I'm sorry, ladies." The doctor held up a hand, stopping Libba and me. "Family only. We're admitting Mrs. George. I'm sure she'd like to see you later today."

Libba planted her hands on her hips. "But—"

My stomach rumbled. I'd skipped dinner last night and missed breakfast this morning. No wonder the poor thing was louder than a midnight freight train.

"Go have some lunch," suggested the doctor. He led Preston toward a set of swinging doors.

"Sorry about this," said Preston. "I'll call you after I've talked to her."

"Give her our love," said Libba.

"Tell her we'll be by this afternoon," I added.

Preston disappeared behind the swinging doors.

"Are you hungry?" asked Libba.

"I am, but I think I'd like to go home." Murder and overdoses were exhausting. Suddenly I didn't have the strength to put a napkin in my lap much less make conversation over a salad.

She nodded. "Me too. I'll take you back to your car."

"Thank you."

We didn't talk much on the way back to her building.

Libba parked and we got out of her car.

"Shall I pick you up later this afternoon?" I asked. "Around three?"

"I'll meet you there."

"Perfect." I walked toward my car.

"Ellison." Libba's voice paused my tired steps. "Thank you for coming."

"That's what friends are for. I'll see you around three."

I sank into the driver's seat and rested my head against the steering wheel. My mind was as jumbled as Grace's bedroom. Khaki and Stan and Phoenix House and something Karen had said. Revolvers and candlesticks and white Mercedes.

I started the ignition and drove home, less than thrilled to be facing a lunch of leftover curry.

I pulled in the driveway and the front door flew open.

A coatless Aggie ran down the front steps. "I've been trying to find you. Thank God you're home."

My lungs constricted and, despite the cold, sweat dampened my skin. "What's wrong?"

"It's Grace."

The sudden furious beating of my heart bruised my chest. "What's happened? Is she all right?"

"She's fine. I promise. She's fine."

"But?"

"She's been arrested."

# FIFTEEN

"Arrested? Grace?" The wind grabbed my questions and sent them out into the street. "For what?"

"Protesting."

"Protesting what?" It took all I had not to scream the question at her.

A sudden gust whipped Aggie's kaftan around her ankles. She crossed one arm over her chest. The other she used to keep her kaftan from flying up. "It's freezing out here. Why don't you come inside?"

"Fine." I climbed out of the car and we dashed into the warm house. Max, who was not a fan of cold weather, waited for me in the foyer. He leaned his head against my leg. His doggy version of a hug. Arrested? I took deep calming breaths and scratched behind Max's ear. Breathe in—Grace wasn't dead. Breathe out—Grace wasn't hurt. "Protesting what?"

Aggie swallowed and ran her fingers from her temples deep into her sproingy hair.

"What? What was she protesting?"

"Your cousin Cora's luncheon."

Oh. Dear. Lord. I closed my eyes and pinched the bridge of my nose. "Why was Grace protesting a charity luncheon?" My voice was even, calm-before-the-storm even.

Poor Aggie. Her fingers appeared to be stuck in her hair. "I don't think it was the luncheon so much as the speaker."

Who was the speaker? Mother had never told me. "Who spoke?"

Aggie looked at the floor, at the ceiling, at me. And with her fingers, or at least a couple of her rings, stuck in her hair, all that looking around looked a lot like the sky was falling. She shifted her gaze back to the ceiling. "Phyllis Schlafly."

"Phyllis Schlafly? The woman who led the campaign against the Equal Rights Amendment?" Disbelief colored my voice. I'd given money to a luncheon that brought that woman in as a speaker? No wonder Mother pussyfooted around telling me who was coming. "I'm going to kill her."

"Phyllis Schlafly?"

"No. Mother. Where's Grace?"

"She and your aunt—"

"My aunt?" I should have guessed that Aunt Sis had a hand in this. "Which police station?" My stomach rumbled. Loudly.

Aggie yanked her hands free. "East."

"East?" Oh dear Lord. Grace was in a sketchy part of town, and my tone when I'd asked where she was sounded exactly like Mother's. Which was worse?

Given that Aggie took a step away from me, probably the tone. "I'm afraid so." She took another step backward. "You must be hungry. Should I make you a sandwich while you change?"

Change? I looked down at my jeans and worn loafers. Aggie was right. I'd be taken more seriously if I showed up at the police station in something other than jeans and a sweater that smelled vaguely of hospital waiting room. The five-minute delay it would cost me to throw on a dress was worth it. "Please. I'd love a sandwich."

Aggie escaped to the kitchen and I hurried up the stairs.

*Brnnng, brnng.*

I eyed the telephone next to my bed. Nope. Not answering. The way my day was going, there was zero possibility the caller had good news. I pulled my sweater over my head, tossed it on the bed, and headed for my closet. A navy dress said responsible, respectable—and I had the perfect one.

*Brnnng, brnng.*

They'd give up eventually. That or Aggie would take a message. I perused the navy section of my closet. A black and white Diane Von Furstenberg print caught my attention and I abandoned my search for blue.

The print dress said responsible, respectable, and of the means to hire every lawyer in the city.

*Brnnng, brn—*

Aggie had answered the phone.

I pulled the dress out of the closet, slid out of my loafers, and shucked off my jeans. Running a brush through my hair wouldn't be amiss.

"Mrs. Russell?" Aggie stood in the doorway. Her voice was tentative. The voice one might use when disturbing a hibernating bear. A large hibernating bear. A grizzly.

"What?" I tried for a pleasant tone and got Mother's icy one instead.

"There's a woman on the phone. Diane Barker. She says she's with the paper."

Diane Barker was the society columnist. What was she calling about? The dead man in my dining room, my overdosed friend, or my jailbird daughter?

"Did you tell her I was busy?"

Aggie nodded. "She insists on speaking with you."

Perfect. "I'll take the call up here. Would you please bring me a cup of coffee?"

Aggie stepped into my bedroom and put a steaming mug into my hands. What would I do without her?

"Aggie, I apologize for being short with you."

"No apology necessary. You're having a rough twenty-four hours."

It was nice of her to make allowances. "I am sorry."

"No need. Take your call." She disappeared into the hallway.

I picked up the receiver. "Hello, Diane. What a pleasure to hear from you."

In general, Diane was a very nice woman. We went to the same high school, belonged to the same country club, and attended some of the same parties. Two things kept us from actual friendship. She was fifteen years older than I was, and she worked for a newspaper. I didn't like seeing my name in the paper.

"I'm surprised I caught you at home," she said. "I thought you'd be at Cora's luncheon."

"I have an opening in New York later this month. I have to get some work done." A half-truth. I did have an opening, but the paintings were already shipped.

"But you hosted the benefactor party." It wasn't a question.

"I did."

"So Stan White was murdered in your home?"

Ugh. Of course she knew about that. "Yes."

"Four days after his wife was murdered in your home."

"Where is this going, Diane?" Mother's tone can be very useful.

"It doesn't look good, Ellison."

"Half the women in this city hired Khaki as a decorator. I can assure you, her death had nothing to do with her being in my home."

"And Mr. White?"

"I don't know why Mr. White was here. I was busy with party guests when he arrived and when he died."

"The party," Diane cooed. "Are you a Phyllis Schlafly fan?"

"No."

"Yet—"

This was going nowhere good, and I had a daughter and an aunt to bail out of jail. "Cora chaired the luncheon. Cora is family. I hosted the party as a favor to my cousin."

"So your family ties are stronger than your convictions?"

The truth was if I'd known the speaker was Phyllis Schlafly I wouldn't have hosted the party. I certainly wouldn't have written a large check to support her appearance. That was probably why Mother hadn't told me. I lowered my head and rubbed my eyes. "No comment."

What I wanted to say was that there was something very

wrong about a woman with a comfortable life espousing the things Phyllis Schlafly did. A woman in an unhappy marriage didn't think it was privilege to be dependent on her husband. That woman was trapped by economics. What kind of job could she get when her resume included raising children and having dinner on the table by six? That woman needed equal rights.

"You're sure?" asked Diane.

"No comment." If I said anything negative about Cora's speaker, Mother would be furious. And she'd be right. Family stuck together. I glanced at the clock on my bedside table. "Diane, I need to run."

"Oh?"

"I'm afraid so." I offered no explanation. I'd done enough damage already. No way was I telling the woman who wrote the society page that half the women in my family were sitting in the pokey waiting for me to bail them out. "Goodbye." I hung up the phone, pulled on the dress, and hurried downstairs.

The police station smelled of burnt coffee and too many bodies packed into an overheated building. I wrinkled my nose.

A woman in a short denim skirt, high heeled boots, and a fake fur jacket rested her elbows on the front desk. It was a posture that gave me an up close and personal view of her barely covered hiney.

"Come on," she said. "Give a girl a break."

A few chairs lined the walls. They made the uncomfortable seats at the hospital seem positively luxurious.

I stood, waiting my turn, and unbuttoned my coat. Lord, it was hot.

The door from the outside opened and a welcome gust of cold air rushed past me.

"Ellison!" Mother's voice was considerably less welcome.

I turned and faced her.

The helmet of her snowy white hair was offset by the deep black of her Persian lamb stroller.

"What are you doing?" she demanded.

"Waiting to talk to someone about Grace and Aunt Sis."

She looked at the woman who was deep in conversation with the desk sergeant and curled her lip.

"I cannot believe Sis did this."

"I can't believe you didn't tell me who the speaker was."

She waved her still-gloved hand. "I didn't think it was important."

I closed my eyes on the red haze that filled my vision.

"I can't get hold of your father. Call Hunter."

Oh dear. "Let's wait and see if we need a lawyer."

Mother snorted. Quietly. "My sister and my granddaughter have been arrested and you want to wait and see if we need a lawyer?" Her voice was low and furious.

"I broke up with Hunter."

"Have. You. Lost. Your. Mind?" The young woman at the desk turned her head and gaped at us. The desk sergeant gaped too. Probably people deep within the bowels of the building were gaping, not sure at what.

"This is neither the time nor the place." I jerked my chin at the woman in the boots. Now that she'd turned to look at us, I saw she was wearing a bikini top under her coat. Wow. Also wow, despite her ensemble, she was the one gaping at us.

Mother, who looked as if she was ready to say much more on the topic, snapped her mouth closed. Maybe it was the shock of the bikini top. Unfortunately, Mother recovered her ability to speak quickly. "I'm calling him anyway."

"Don't."

"Pardon me?"

"Don't call Hunter." I kept my voice low. Mother's and my problems were not meant for sharing. "Let's see if we can handle this on our own before we call for reinforcements."

Mother stared at me as if I was speaking gibberish.

"Don't call him, Mother."

We stared at each other—scowled really. Two women caught in

an epic battle of wills. Or at least two stubborn women unwilling to give an inch.

The bikini top in November woman turned back to the desk sergeant. "Please?"

"I can't do anything for you," he said.

"Jerk!" The woman in the boots flounced past us.

"How can I help you ladies?" The man behind the desk, with his droopy mustache, too full lips, and straining uniform, looked as though he preferred *not* helping. And if he wouldn't help a girl in a bikini, Mother and I didn't have a snowball's chance in hell of garnering his assistance.

I stepped forward. Smiled. "Good afternoon. My daughter and my aunt were brought in. I'm here to take them home."

He snorted. "The protest, right?"

"Yes."

"The judge hasn't set bail yet."

Oh dear. "What are the charges?"

"Disturbing the peace."

"I told you we needed a lawyer."

I didn't acknowledge Mother's comment. Instead, I smiled at the sergeant. "My daughter is sixteen, a minor. She's never been in any kind of trouble before. Can't you just drop the charges?"

"Not up to me, lady."

I gritted my teeth behind my smile. "May I please speak to the person who can drop the charges?"

"He's busy."

"I'm calling Hunter."

"Mother. Wait." I peered at the man's name tag. "I'm sure Sergeant Decker will be able to help us."

"Nothing I can do." Sergeant Decker crossed his arms over the broad expanse of his belly and leaned back in his chair.

"I'd like to speak with the arresting officer." I turned to Mother. "Maybe you should call Daddy. I bet he can get the police commissioner on the phone." Take that, Sergeant Obstructionist Decker.

Mother inclined her chin to the left and raised her right eyebrow. "No, dear. He can't call. Today's their golf day. They're already together."

Thank God, Mother had read my ploy. I manufactured a shiver. "It's too cold for golf. I bet they're having drinks at the club. If we call the men's grill we can get Uncle Jim on the phone ourselves." I smiled at the sergeant again. "He's not really my uncle. I've just known him so long I call him that."

"Should we use that phone over there?" Mother pointed to a payphone she would never touch, not even with her gloves on.

"I've got change." I plunked my Chanel handbag down on the sergeant's desk, dug for coins, and triumphantly produced a dime. "Sergeant, what's your first name? So I can tell Uncle Jimmy." If I ever called Jim Graham *Uncle Jimmy* he'd probably have me arrested. Sergeant Decker did not need to know that.

"Wait." The sergeant held up his hands. "Let me see if I can find you someone to talk to."

"Are you sure? It's no trouble to call the club." I held two fingers to my chin and looked at the water-stained ceiling. "You know, now that I think about it, we should probably talk to whoever is in charge."

"Just give me a minute, ma'am." He picked up the phone and spoke low and fast.

Mother and I exchanged a look—we'd worked together and got something we both wanted. A first. Both the working together and the wanting the same thing.

We waited. Standing. Mother unwilling to risk her Persian lamb for the dubious comforts of the chairs that lined the walls. I didn't blame her. There was no way my camel hair was going near their stained surfaces.

A woman with teased hair and blue eyeshadow emerged from the door behind Sergeant Decker. "This way please."

We followed her into a squad room. Women—bell-bottom-wearing nature girls, mothers in twin sets and loafers, grandmotherly types wearing too bright coral lipstick with hair like cotton balls—occupied chairs next to all the desks. This was who the police had decided to arrest?

Grace and Aunt Sis sat together at a disreputable desk, their backs to the door.

My daughter and my aunt turned in unison. I'd like to think they turned because they felt my stare burning into the back of their fool heads. I'd like to believe that, but I was pretty sure it was Mother's stare that singed the hair on their napes.

"Let's get them out of here." I spoke through gritted teeth. "We can kill them later."

# SIXTEEN

The policeman sitting across the desk from my aunt and daughter had caterpillars hanging over his eyes. Deep lines etched his face from the sides of his nose to the corners of his mouth. He'd loosened his tie and collar and rolled up his sleeves. He looked bone tired.

He pressed a phone between his right ear and shoulder and took notes with his left hand, nodding from time to time as if the person on the other end could see him.

"Yes, sir. I understand, sir. No problem." He hung up the phone and rubbed his forehead as if he had a headache.

He probably did. And it was probably from all the smoke.

Smoke rose from countless cigarettes and the heat was damp and close.

The air was as fresh as daisies when compared to the *energy* in the room...I wasn't the only one to notice that men sat on the business side of the desks, that men had arrested women who were demanding equal rights.

The policeman fixed his dark gaze on Aunt Sis. "You ladies are free to go."

For a half-second I wondered if Anarchy had been on the other end of that phone call.

Ridiculous.

Anarchy believed in rules. And consequences.

Aunt Sis and Grace had broken the rules. If it was up to him, there would be consequences.

Whoever had okayed Aunt Sis and Grace's release had to be a friend of my father's.

Aunt Sis crossed her arms and leaned back in her chair.

"We're not going anywhere. Not as long as you're holding everyone else."

"For heaven's sake, Sis." Mother turned Aunt Sis' name into a furious hiss. "Someone has to be the first to leave. None of these women will be here long."

Mother was right. Even the nature girls looked like they had bail money.

"Let's go. Before they change their minds and decide to charge you." I jerked my chin toward the door.

Grace leapt from her chair. Eager to return home or eager to escape the full ashtrays and pervasive scent of smoke? It didn't matter as long as we were leaving.

Sis sighed and stood.

We walked to the exit and I made mental notes. Mother was mad at all of us. I was mad at Aunt Sis and Grace...and Mother. She should have told me Phyllis Schlafly was the speaker. Aunt Sis was angry with Mother and possibly me. The ride home was going to be a barrel of fun.

We paused outside the police station, glad of the gusts of chilled wind. Glad of air that didn't reek of cigarettes.

"My house or yours?" Mother's lips and nose and eyes were pinched with unexpressed emotion. She looked ready to kill someone. Me or Aunt Sis? Maybe both of us?

"Yours." There had been enough murders at my house already.

"I'll take Sis. You drive Grace."

I wasn't about to argue over details.

"Mrs. Russell!"

I turned.

Detective Peters hurried toward us, his shoes crunching the dirty snow on the sidewalk. "What are you doing here?"

"Who is that?" whispered Aunt Sis.

"Anarchy's partner," I whispered back.

He stopped in front of us and waited for an answer.

"There was a misunderstanding at a luncheon today. We

cleared things up." Mother's voice made it clear further questions were unwelcome.

Detective Peters ignored Mother's verbal hint. "Who got arrested?"

"I did," said Sis.

"And you are?"

"My aunt. We're done here. Have a nice afternoon, detective."

"I have a few more questions about last night."

Of course he did. "Now is not a good time."

"I'll come by your house later." Was that a threat?

"Call first. I'm very busy."

There was the scowl he reserved just for me. The one that made his brow look like crumpled newspaper and narrowed his eyes to slits. "I'll do that."

The wind suddenly seemed much colder—no longer refreshing, instead, bone-chilling.

We hurried to the cars. Grace rode with me. Aunt Sis rode with Mother.

Grace climbed into the passenger's seat. "Can't we just go home?"

"It's better to get it over with."

"How mad is she?"

"Scale of one to ten?" I asked.

Grace nodded.

"Eleven. Maybe twelve."

Grace slumped in her seat with her arms crossed. "How mad are you?"

"With you? Five." I slowed for a stoplight.

"Really?" She sounded almost hopeful.

The car came to a stop, and I turned and looked at her. "You skipped school."

"Aunt Sis wrote a note."

I pondered that. "She signed my name?"

Grace kept her gaze pinned to the windshield. "Yes." A small sound but a truthful one.

The car behind me honked. The light was green. I pressed on the accelerator. "You're grounded for the weekend."

"Mooooom. No. That's so unfair. I had to protest that woman."

"I'm not grounding you for protesting. I'm grounding you for skipping school."

"Like you would have let me go."

"I would have."

"Really?" She sounded surprised.

"Really."

"But the party."

"I didn't know who the speaker was."

"Really?" Now she sounded disbelieving.

"There's been a lot going on." Finding a new body every four days could be very distracting.

"If you say so."

We drove in silence for a few blocks, then she added, "Please don't be mad at Aunt Sis."

I shifted my gaze from the road ahead to my daughter. Was she serious?

"I would have gone without her."

"Be that as it may."

I didn't have to be looking at her to know she rolled her eyes.

We pulled up to the curb in front of Mother's house but neither of us opened our doors.

"This is going to be bad, isn't it?" Grace asked.

"Think Guernica."

"The painting by Picasso?"

"Yes, but also the town. Guernica was bombed to near rubble by the Nazis."

"She's that mad?"

I closed my fingers around the door handle. "She's that mad." I opened the door and added, "But so am I."

We marched up the front walk and rang the bell.

Penelope answered the door. "Your mother isn't home, Mrs. Russell."

"She will be." I sounded grim.

We stepped into the foyer and Grace looked up at the gaping hole in the ceiling. "Wow."

"It's been a rough week. For all of us."

"Should I make coffee?" asked Penelope.

"That's an excellent idea. Thank you."

"May I take your wraps?"

"We'll keep them with us." We'd need our coats if we had to make a speedy escape. "Grace and I will wait for Mother in the living room."

We didn't wait long. I was just laying my coat over the back of the sofa when Mother and Aunt Sis marched in. They looked as stiff and uncompromising as the shafts of nine-irons. Obviously they'd had words in the car.

Mother's gimlet gaze bounced between me and Grace. Eeny, meeny, miny, moe..."Ellison, what do you mean you broke things off with Hunter?" I was the winner, the first to receive her ire.

"Who I date is none of your business." Calm. Reasonable.

"It's as if you don't want to be happy." Either Mother hadn't heard me or, more likely, my assertion that who I dated was none of her damned business wasn't worth considering.

"Now, Frannie, Ellison doesn't need a man to be happy." Aunt Sis' intentions were good—maybe. Statements like that were like throwing gasoline on a fire.

"Your sister and granddaughter were arrested, and you're mad at me for breaking up with Hunter?" This wasn't exactly a surprise.

"They're out of jail. The charges are dropped. You won't get another chance to catch a man like Hunter."

"So be it." It was time to go on the offensive. "How could you neglect to tell me that the speaker at Cora's luncheon was Phyllis Schlafly?"

For an instant—less than a blink of an eye—Mother's expression shifted from controlled fury to guilt. "Don't be ridiculous. I assumed you knew." Mother scratched the end of her nose.

Itchy noses when lying were a family curse.

"You did not."

"Of course I did."

"You had me host a party for that woman. Thank God her plane was delayed."

"There's nothing wrong with Phyllis. She's a lovely woman." Mother had a tough audience for comments like that.

Aunt Sis snorted. Grace rolled her eyes. And I guffawed.

Mother was losing an argument, an occurrence as rare as Haley's Comet. Unlike Haley's Comet, Mother had the ability to change course. "You two—" her gaze encompassed Aunt Sis and Grace "—have behaved shamefully."

Aunt Sis raised an unconcerned brow. Grace swallowed audibly.

"No matter how you feel about Phyllis, that was your cousin's luncheon. Family comes first."

The arch of Aunt Sis' brow slipped.

"You—" Mother pointed at Grace "—will apologize to your cousin for disrupting her luncheon."

"But—"

"No buts, young lady."

"I'll go with you, Grace. You can explain *why* you protested. And I'll tell Cora that if I'd known what you were doing, I would have been there with you."

Aunt Sis closed the space between us and draped her arm over my shoulders. "We would have asked you to join us, but with two murders on your plate, we assumed you were busy."

"Sis, I'd like a word." Mother looked angry enough to spit golf tees.

My aunt seemed unconcerned. She waved us toward the front door and escape. "I'll talk to you later."

Maybe. If Mother didn't kill her.

We slipped outside and climbed into the car.

I stuck the key in the ignition. "Do you want to get it over with?"

Grace tilted her head. "Get what over with?"

"Apologizing to Cora."

Her teenage jaw dropped. "Wait. You're actually going to make me do that?"

"I am. She's your cousin."

"Aunt Sis doesn't have to apologize."

"She doesn't have to, but she will." Maybe.

"Fine," Grace huffed.

I drove the few blocks to Cora and Thornton's and parked.

"What do I say?" asked Grace.

"Tell her it wasn't your intention to disrupt her luncheon." I offered up an encouraging smile.

Grace caught her lower lip in her teeth. "What if she's mad at me?"

"What if she is?"

"I hate it when people are mad at me."

I'd spent most of my life feeling that way. It hadn't gotten me far. "All you can do is apologize and ask for her forgiveness." I stared out the windshield. The sullen gray of the street matched the sky. "It wouldn't hurt to tell her how strongly you feel about women's rights so she knows you didn't do this on a lark."

Grace squared her shoulders and opened the passenger's door. "Let's get this over with."

The wind propelled us toward the front door. I rang the bell and we waited.

And waited.

Another gust buffeted our backs and still we waited.

"Isn't that Cousin Cora's car in the drive?" Grace pointed to a gold Cutlass.

"It is. And that's Thornton's Mercedes behind it." I rang the bell a second time.

Grace jammed her hands in her pockets. "They're not here."

The door flew open and a red-faced Thornton glared at us. With his tie askew and his hair mussed, he looked slightly deranged. "What?" More than *slightly* deranged.

Grace took a step back.

I held my ground. "We'd like to see Cora."

"Cora doesn't want to see anyone."

"Grace would like to apologize."

Thornton stared at us.

Another gust of wind assaulted us. And him. And Thornton wasn't wearing a coat.

"Fine. Come in." He stood back from the door, and Grace and I hurried inside.

"I'll tell Cora you're here." Thornton left us standing in the foyer.

"He's really mad," Grace whispered.

I didn't argue.

A moment later, Cora shuffled into the front hall with Thornton behind her. She looked twenty years older than she had last night. She moved as if she ached and her eyes were red-rimmed.

"Cousin Cora, are you all right?" Grace took a step toward her cousin and reached out her hand.

Cora looked at Grace's hand as if it belonged to a leper. "I'm fine. Thornton said you wanted to apologize."

"I do. I'm so sorry if I upset you or disrupted your luncheon."

"You should be." Thornton glared at her.

"Thornton, might I trouble you for a cup of coffee?"

"Coffee?"

"Wonderful beverage," I said. "Hot and full of caffeine."

"I'll make some," said Cora.

"No, no. You stay here and talk to Grace. I'm sure Thornton can show me where everything is." Thornton probably didn't know what a coffee filter was, much less where to find one, but I wanted Grace to have the chance to make her apology without him interrupting.

I stepped forward and laid my hand on his arm. "The kitchen?"

"Fine." He said the word grudgingly. "This way."

I followed him down the hallway to a kitchen that was bright and cheery despite the dreary weather outside.

"This is lovely," I said. "Khaki designed this?"

"It cost a fortune." He pointed at a Mr. Coffee. "There's the coffeemaker."

"I don't usually drink coffee so late in the day, but it's so cold out and—"

Again, he pointed. "She keeps the stuff in the cabinet."

The stuff. Coffee and filters. I put a filter in Mr. Coffee, scooped grounds, and added water to his reservoir.

Thornton sat at the kitchen table and watched me.

"What a gorgeous table."

"It should be. It could have belonged to a president for what I paid for it."

Thornton had many faults, but I'd never counted being cheap among them. Or maybe he wasn't being cheap, maybe complaining about the high price was his way of highlighting his ability to pay.

"I'm sure it's worth every penny."

He snorted.

Mr. Coffee diligently filled his pot.

Of the two men in the kitchen, I knew which one I preferred.

"Grace and Sis didn't mean to disrupt Cora's luncheon."

Thornton scowled. "I don't know why I ever thought she could pull something like that off."

"How did Cora pick the speaker?"

Thornton shifted in his chair as if it had suddenly become uncomfortable.

"Not that I'm judging, but Phyllis Schlafly was bound to be controversial." I needed to shut up. The scowl on Thornton's face was deepening with every word I said.

"I suggested Mrs. Schlafly."

"You don't support women's rights?" It was like poking a bear. I knew better. I knew better and I did it anyway.

"Hell no. Most women are just like Cora—in need of a firm hand."

"Mother would be surprised to hear you say that." That sounded so much better than *you are a chauvinist pig. No. Ass. You are a chauvinist ass.*

"Your mother is an exception. She's a fine woman."

And Cora wasn't? Cora was his wife.

Mr. Coffee finished dripping. I pulled three mugs out of the cabinet and poured coffee into one of them. "Do you take cre—?" What was I doing? I was a guest in his house, but because I was a woman I was serving him?

"The cream's in the fridge." Thornton pointed at the refrigerator. Thornton was big on pointing. My back stiffened and I bit my tongue.

I'd come here to apologize, not instigate more family drama. I suppressed the urge to pour hot coffee in Thornton's lap, fetched the cream, added a dollop to his cup, and handed it to him.

He didn't thank me.

Next I poured coffee into the other two cups. "Does Cora take cream?"

His brows lifted as if the question surprised him. "I don't know."

They'd been married how many years?

"You think your daughter's done apologizing?"

I took a sip of coffee. It didn't taste as good as the coffee at my house. A bitter taste lingered. "I'll go check."

Thornton pushed away from the table. "I'll come with you." His meaning was clear. He wanted us gone.

We walked down the hall to the foyer and heard voices coming from the living room.

"I hope I'm not interrupting—" I held up the mug I'd poured for Cora "—but I brought you coffee."

"You're not interrupting." Cora's voice was faint.

"Here." I put the mug into her hands. "You sound as if you could use this."

Cora took a sip and made a face.

"I'm sorry. I wasn't sure if you took cream or sugar."

"Both." She took another sip and offered me a sickly smile. "But this tastes wonderful."

"Cora, you look as if you should lie down." An understatement. That she was standing was a miracle. She was beyond pale and the hands holding her coffee mug were shaking. "We'll get out of your hair."

"I am really sorry, Cousin Cora." Grace sounded genuinely contrite.

Behind me, Thornton made a low noise, suspiciously close to a growl.

I had all I could take of Thornton. "Let's go, Grace."

"I'll see you out," said Cora.

"Don't be silly. We'll see ourselves out. You go rest."

Grace and I stepped outside and were met with rain mixed with ice. We hurried to the car.

I turned on the ignition and the heat.

"Cousin Cora..." Grace's voice trailed off.

"Cousin Cora what?" I pulled away from the curb.

"Are you sure she's okay?"

No. "Why do you ask?"

"She flinched when I hugged her."

"Sometimes when people are upset, they feel it in their muscles and bones."

Grace did not look convinced. I didn't blame her.

"She flinched as if I'd hurt her," Grace insisted. "I didn't even squeeze."

"We'll check on her tomorrow." I gazed out the windshield at the horrible weather. "I've got to go and visit Jinx in the hospital."

"In the hospital? What's wrong with her?"

Whoops. I rubbed the end of my nose in anticipation of the itch. "Food poisoning."

"But she ate at our house last night."

I drove slowly, all too aware of the ice pellets hitting the street and how poorly the Triumph handled in inclement weather. "How do you know that?"

"I heard her voice."

"Really? There were a lot of voices."

"Only when everybody was getting there. This was later. She was telling Mr. George to get out of the dining room."

The car hit a patch of ice and spun. With one hand I clutched the wheel, turning into the skid. The other arm flew in front of Grace, blocking her from hitting the windshield.

We completed a circle and came to a stop.

Neither of us said a word. I, for one, couldn't. My heart was too firmly lodged in my throat. My mouth was as dry as a sand trap in August, there was a real possibility my left hand was fused to the steering wheel, and the slick pavement in front of us appeared to be at the end of a tunnel.

"Are you all right?" Grace spoke first.

I nodded. "You?"

"Fine. Maybe you should go see Mrs. George tomorrow."

I nodded again. It had been a long day. Jinx would understand. And I'd have questions for her. So many questions.

"Do you want me to drive?"

That was just what I needed. To be stressed and tired and in the passenger seat with a teenager behind the wheel during an ice storm. There was a lot to be said for being in control. "No. I'm fine. Let's go home."

# SEVENTEEN

The institutional white of the sheet that covered Jinx turned the vestiges of her summer tan a jaundiced yellow.

Her face, wiped clean of makeup, looked older and softer and sadder. Her eyes were closed. Was she sleeping?

I paused just inside the door, clutching a copy of Joseph Heller's new book, *Something Happened*, and a bag of pastries from the patisserie on the Plaza.

The window sill held two enormous arrangements of roses. Hot house roses. No floral scent combatted the smell of hospital.

Jinx's eyelids fluttered open. "Ellison."

I stepped all the way into the room. "How are you feeling?"

"Like hell." She shifted her gaze to the window, sleet pinged against the glass. Her lips thinned. "They pumped my stomach."

I was torn between sympathy and a desire to throttle her. She had scared Libba and me half to death. But she looked so pale, no makeup, and her hair a mess that sympathy won.

"That sounds horrible. I don't suppose you want these?" I held up the bag of croissants. Why hadn't I thought about her stomach? I should have brought flowers or a plant.

"Are you kidding? As soon as I'm cleared for solids, I'm eating every single morsel in that bag. They don't feed you in this place."

I put the bag down on the L-shaped table next to her bed. "I also brought you this." I held up the book then added it to the table. "It's a new bestseller." Jinx liked staying *au courant* with the latest books.

"*Something Happened*," she read out loud. "It sure as hell did."

"What? What happened?" I took off my coat and sank into the chair next to her bed. Many naugas had given their hydes for that chair. It made an embarrassing squeaking sound as my bottom met its surface.

We giggled. Nervous, avoid-the-elephant-in-the-room giggles.

There wasn't enough *room* in the room for an elephant. "I mean it." I shifted my gaze to my friend in the hospital bed. "What happened?"

Her gaze slid back to the window, a mere pane of glass protecting us from the elements. "I took too many pills."

She made it sound as if she'd miscounted. How did that happen? Why was she taking any pills at all? "Why?"

"I didn't do it on purpose." Now she sounded peevish. "It just...happened. I made a mistake."

I wasn't buying it.

"Who was it that said there are no mistakes?"

She gave up on watching the weather and settled her tired gaze on me. "Freud. But he was a misogynistic ass." Jinx had studied psychology in college—Freud and Jung and Lord knew who else. To argue with her meant an hours-long discussion. Besides, for all I knew, Freud might have been a misogynist. I kept quiet.

I looked down at my lap again. I wore gray flannel pants. One of Max's hairs had migrated to the fabric and I picked the tiny length of soft gray off my leg and let it drift into the trash can. "What happened on Thursday night?"

The air in the room stilled. The only sounds were the low hum of machinery, the encroaching weather, and the distant voices of a few nurses.

"Nothing." The pitch of Jinx's voice was high—squeaky high—and her cheeks paled until they were whiter than the bleached sheets. Any idiot could tell she was lying.

"The truth." I clasped my hands in my lap, ready for the worst. "Please."

Jinx stared at the ceiling. Hardly scintillating. "I don't know how you do it."

"Do what?"

She rubbed her eyes. "Find bodies."

"I don't do it on purpose." No matter what Mother thought, that was God's truth.

"Neither did we."

The hospital sounds, the roses that didn't smell, the naugahyde waiting to rub against my bottom and make another rude noise—they all faded away. "You found Stan?"

Jinx's nod was barely perceptible. "Preston wanted another egg." She shuddered. "Why did you serve those awful things?"

Why had Preston wanted a second one? That was a better question.

"Mother picked the buffet items." Under normal circumstances we would have commiserated over Mother selecting the menu at *my* house. These weren't normal circumstances. "About Stan?"

"I went with Preston to get the egg and we saw him." Her eyes widened as if she could actually see Stan on my dining room floor, the pool of blood, the candlestick, the *matter*. She crossed her arms over her chest. "It was awful."

No argument. "Why didn't you go for help?"

"We panicked." She squeezed her eyes closed. "I'd spent the past few weeks telling my friends that Khaki overcharged for services. I told them she broke up her clients' marriages. I told them to watch their own husbands. And now Khaki's husband was dead." A single tear escaped her shuttered lids. "One of us—both of us—would have been suspects. We saw Stan there on the floor and we froze."

"Froze?"

She nodded emphatically. Even opened her eyes and stared at me as if I'd be able to read the truth in her irises.

"And then?"

A few more tears meandered down her cheeks. Could I believe in those tears?

She wiped her eyes with the backs of her hands. "We turned

out the lights and left him. We went back to the living room and acted as if nothing happened."

The person who'd killed Stan had done the same thing—returned to the living room or the family room, reclaimed their plate or drink, and pretended like nothing happened.

"I couldn't sleep Thursday night. I saw Stan every time I closed my eyes, so I took a few pills. Preston woke me yesterday morning and told me I had to act normally. He went to work. I sat at my kitchen table and got more and more anxious. So I took more pills."

I withheld judgment. Sort of. Surely she could find a better way to handle stress than valium.

"I can tell what you're thinking, Ellison, and I don't have a problem with drugs."

"I didn't say a word."

"You didn't have to," she snapped. "Besides, they're not *drugs*. They're prescription medication."

It wasn't an argument I'd win. "Why did you go to Libba's?"

"It made sense at the time. Libba and I were supposed to have lunch, and I was trying to lead a normal day."

Normal? By showing up at Libba's at nine in the morning zonked out of her mind? Or had Jinx counted on the fact that of all her friends, Libba, who seldom rose before ten, was the one guaranteed to be home, to get her help? Was Jinx that calculating?

"Did you see anything on Thursday night? Anyone in the front hall?"

"You mean before we found Stan?"

No, before the caterer served coffee. "Yes, before you found Stan."

"There was no one around." The words came so fast they tumbled over each other.

I sat in silence, thinking. My friend was addicted to pills. My friend found a corpse in my dining room and left it there. My friend might be a killer.

"If you don't believe me, ask Preston."

I intended to. I stood. "I'll let you rest."

"Ellison." Jinx's voice was as raw as the weather outside. "You and Libba saved me. Thank you."

I leaned over and kissed her cheek. "You're welcome."

The parking garage at the hospital was a country mile from the patients' rooms. The walk gave me time to think.

About Jinx and Preston. I had to talk to Preston.

About Khaki.

About Stan.

About...The conversation I had with Karen still niggled at me. Everyone told me that Khaki had a tendency to overcharge. The fact that many of her clients' marriages ended in divorce was indisputable. Yet Karen, who was presumably overcharged and had seen her marriage end, adored Khaki. Why?

This had to stop. I was running out of rooms for people to be murdered in.

Karen didn't live far away—one of the poet apartment buildings on the Plaza. Was it the Robert Browning or the Washington Irving? Maybe the Henry Wadsworth? I pictured the page in the Junior League directory. She lived in the Washing Irving. Fifth floor. I was sure of it.

I drove to the Plaza, parked in front of her building, and, gathering my coat around me and sinking my neck into its collar, negotiated the frozen concrete of the front steps.

No door man. Just a locked door.

I found Karen's name on the list of buttons next to the door and pushed.

Nothing.

I poked at the button a second time.

"That's not working." A young man in a leather jacket and jaunty scarf pushed the door open from the inside. He jerked his goateed chin at the open door. "Go on in."

I went and was grateful for the wave of warmth that welcomed me.

Five-twelve.

Karen's building was not luxurious, but it had a certain old-world charm. A charm that mixed well the scents of aged iron (the bannisters) and ancient carpet. The elevator looked as ancient as the carpet. I climbed the stairs. Five flights. This place was a far cry from the home Karen had shared with her husband in Sunset Hills.

I stopped at the top of the stairs. The landing was dim. And quiet.

Five-twelve.

Down the hall.

I knocked and the door swung open.

Dread seeped into the hallway, wrapped around my ankles, and twined its way up my legs. My heart, which was already beating at a decent clip after five flights of stairs, sped up. A sinking feeling lowered my stomach to my knees. "Karen?" My voice shook.

No answer.

I stuck my head inside the apartment. There was no foyer. The front door opened directly into the living room. Or what had been the living room.

A porcelain lamp had been smashed into shards, an upholstered chair was upended, and there was blood. Everywhere. Painting the lamp's shards. Splashed on the wall. Spattered across the floor.

"Karen?" I yelled this time.

No answer.

The idiot girl in the horror movie who goes into the dark house where the axe murderer hides—the one about whom every woman in the audience is silently thinking, "No loss. She's too stupid to live." That was me.

Except it wasn't a creepy house. It was a mid-priced apartment. It wasn't dark. I saw all too well the potential danger. And it wasn't some imaginary kid in peril. It was a real woman. Me. "Karen?"

I stepped into the living room

Did the idiot girls get not-alone, creepy-crawly feelings on the backs of their necks? The kind of feeling that trickled down their spines and tightened every nerve. I sure did.

The smart thing to do was go to another apartment and ask to use the phone. I was not too stupid to live.

I backed toward the hallway.

A moan stopped me in my tracks.

"Karen?"

"Help." The word was faint, barely a word.

But I'd heard it. There was no backing out now.

"Karen?" I stepped into the living room and climbed over a ladder back chair that had been reduced to matchsticks.

"Help." The voice came from the next room.

I rounded the corner and stopped.

Holy Mother of God. I covered my mouth—a futile attempt at stemming sudden nausea. I swallowed, breathed through my mouth, closed my eyes. After a few seconds, the storm in my stomach subsided.

I opened my eyes.

I'd seen dead people that looked better than Karen Fleming.

Her face was so swollen and purple it hardly looked like a face. Her left leg bent at an odd angle and there was blood. So much blood it seemed impossible that there could be any left in her body. I knelt next to her and took her hand. "Hang in there. I'll call for help."

The telephone was on the floor next to me, ripped from the wall.

"Is there a phone in your bedroom?"

She didn't answer me.

"We need help." Mistress of the obvious, that was me.

She didn't answer me. Imagine that.

I released her hand and rushed down the short length of the only hallway. The bedroom had to be at the end.

The place where Karen laid her head at night was untouched. The bed neatly made. Her brush set placed with precision on the dresser. A phone sat on the nightstand.

I snatched the receiver from the cradle and dialed *the* number.

Anarchy answered on the first ring. "Jones."

"It's Ellison." My lungs refused to fully inflate. "I'm at Karen Fleming's and she's been attacked."

"Who is Karen Fleming?" He sounded cool and calm and in control—all the things I wasn't.

"She was a friend of Khaki's."

"What's the address?"

"The Washington Irving apartments. Number five-twelve. Anarchy—" I swallowed the lump in my throat. "I'm afraid she may die."

"I'll send an ambulance, and I'm on my way." He hung up.

"Hello?" The voice, a woman's, came from the living room.

I hurried down the hall.

Mary Beth Brewer stood just inside the door, clutching the strap of her handbag with both hands as if it was the lifeline that kept her from drowning. "Oh my God, Ellison, what happened?"

I swallowed before I spoke. "Karen was attacked."

Mary Beth stumbled backward. "Where is she?"

"The kitchen. She's...I just called the police."

"She's dead?" Mary Beth's skin turned as white as the paint on the walls. "She can't be dead. We're supposed to have lunch."

"She's not dead." And she wasn't going to lunch.

Mary Beth shook her head as if her neck was a metronome. Side to side. Side to side. "We have lunch on Saturdays during football season. Every Saturday."

"Maybe you should sit down." The poor woman was obviously in shock—beyond shock. She looked as if she was ready to shatter like Karen's porcelain lamp. At least the couch was in one piece; I pointed at it.

"I need to see her." She didn't move. "*He* did this."

He? "Who?"

"Her ex-husband."

"It could have been a robber." It wasn't. I knew it. The attack on Karen was too vicious. Too personal. But I didn't want to believe a man who'd once stood in front of a minister and vowed to love, honor, and protect could do this.

"No. Not a robber." Mary Beth stumbled over the broken chair. "Karen didn't have anything to steal. It was Daniel." She pushed past me, stopping abruptly at the entrance to the kitchen, presumably as frozen by horror as I had been. She grabbed onto the door frame. "Oh my God."

"Why would Daniel do this?"

Mary Beth turned her head and stared at me as if she couldn't believe I'd asked such a stupid question. "Because she left him."

"Women leave their husbands all the time."

Mary Beth's eyes drooped. Her shoulders drooped. The corners of her mouth drooped. She looked twenty years older than she had when she walked through the front door. "Not husbands like Karen's."

"You have to tell the police."

"The police?"

"They're on their way."

"I can't." The metronome-like shaking of her head returned. She loosened her hold on the door frame and backed away from the kitchen.

"But—"

"I can't! Daniel and my husband are friends. They golf. They watch football. They go hunting. I can't tell the police. I can't." She picked her way through the wreckage of the living room.

"I thought you and Karen were friends."

That stopped her.

For a half-second. "Karen would understand."

"Then I'll tell them."

She stopped again. "Please, Ellison." Her brow puckered and she held her splayed fingers against her cheeks and mouth. If I couldn't smell the fear on her skin, she'd have looked comical.

"But—"

"You can't tell anyone I was here. I'm begging you."

"But—"

"Please." Tears filled her eyes. "Pete and I just worked things out. I don't want to rock the boat."

"Fine." Giving in felt wrong, but she was crying. "I'll keep your secret, but—"

With my assurance that I wouldn't tell the police, Mary Beth wasn't interested in *buts*. "You promise?"

Idiot that I was, I nodded.

"I have to go. I can't be here." She slipped through the front door, closing it softly behind her.

Dammit. Was Mary Beth worried Karen's husband would come after her? The destroyed furniture that littered the floor offered no answers. I returned to the kitchen, knelt next to Karen, picked up her limp hand, and waited.

Only a few minutes passed until I heard sirens.

"Ellison?" The sound of Anarchy's voice coming from the living room soothed some of the tension from my shoulders.

"In here."

He appeared in the doorway and the starch that had been keeping me upright dissolved. A tear ran down my cheek and my jaw ached with unspent sobs.

If my expression was grief-stricken, Anarchy's was all cop. Lips in a thin line, eyes narrowed, and a diamond hard cast to his forehead.

A man I didn't know stepped around Anarchy and joined me on the floor. He claimed the hand I held and checked for a pulse. "She's still alive. Would you give me some room, ma'am?"

"Of course." I rose from the floor.

Anarchy closed his warm hand around my elbow, led me to the living room, and sat me on the couch. He even took a seat next to me. "Tell me what happened."

I told him about finding Karen, about calling for help. I even added, "I've heard that Karen and her ex-husband had an acrimonious divorce."

"Where did you hear that?"

"Around." Could he tell I was avoiding his question?

"That's it?"

"That's it."

"Let's get you out of here."

We walked out into the hallway where a small crowd had gathered. An attractive woman stepped forward. "Is Karen all right?"

"Who are you, ma'am?" asked Anarchy.

"I'm Joanne Graham, Karen's next door neighbor."

"Did you see or hear anything unusual this morning?"

"No. But I just got home from a trip a little while ago. My flight was delayed because of the weather." She tilted her head. "Although, I did see someone leaving her apartment when I got off the elevator."

My heart sank.

"When was that?"

"Just before the sirens."

Anarchy turned his cop gaze on me.

This was going to be fun to explain. Not.

# EIGHTEEN

"You lied to me," Anarchy whispered, the angry roar of a Camaro looking to win a race was all too evident in his voice.

"I didn't actually lie." I'd lied by omission. "And I told you everything she told me."

"Oh?" One dangerous, engine-revving word.

"I told you exactly what she said. Daniel Fleming may have done this."

Anarchy grabbed my wrist and pulled me over near the window, away from the paramedics and ambulance personnel. "Who is *she*?"

"Someone who doesn't want to get involved."

"It's a bit late for that."

I looked out the window. The freezing rain had stopped. For now. "She asked me to keep her out of this and I promised I would."

"I could arrest you for interfering with a police investigation."

I pulled my wrist free of his grasp and shook my head. Obstinate? Me? Probably, but I'd promised Mary Beth. "I gave her my word."

"This is an attempted homicide investigation."

"She arrived after I did—after I called you. She has nothing to do with the attack on Karen."

"You protect people who don't deserve your protection."

"How do you know what she does and doesn't deserve? It's not as if you have to go home and explain to your husband why you ratted out his friend."

Anarchy opened his mouth. Another furious reprimand ready

on his lips. But instead of berating me, he snapped his mouth closed with an audible click of his teeth.

Had he seen reason?

"Does he hit her?"

What? "Who?"

"Your mysterious friend. Does her husband hit her?"

"No! Of course not." I rubbed my face with my hands and stared at the slightly worn carpet. I looked up and said, "You have to understand. She's totally dependent on him. She doesn't have any money." Anarchy would never know about asking for a few dollars back when writing a check to the grocery store just to have cash in his pocket. He didn't have to justify the purchase of a new blouse or new underwear. "If he's angry—"

"She doesn't get to go out to lunch with her friends?" His desire to catch a killer was getting in the way of his seeing my point. "She could get a job."

"Doing what? Spritzing perfume at a cosmetics counter?" Women like Mary Beth, who'd spent their lives raising children and doing volunteer work, didn't have a plethora of job skills.

We glared at each other.

I blinked first. "I can't tell you. I can't."

He crossed his arms.

"But—" I crossed my arms too "—I may know something about Khaki's death."

"You think this is related?"

"I don't see how it could be." Khaki's murder had been clinical, almost sterile. What had happened to Karen was messy and awful and spoke of unchecked rage.

"What do you know?"

"Khaki was involved in a charity called Phoenix House. It keeps coming up."

Anarchy lowering his brow and deepening his scowl was not what I expected. I'd been hoping for something more along the lines of *thanks, Ellison! I'll investigate that immediately* followed by a pat on the back—or a peck on the cheek.

"What do you know about Phoenix House?"

He sounded angrier than ever—the Camaro's engine was about to throw a rod. I wasn't sure what that meant—I just knew it was bad.

"Nothing really." I glanced around the dim landing. What can of worms had I opened now?

The medics wheeled a gurney out of Karen's apartment and loaded it onto the elevator. The doors slid closed behind them.

"What are you doing today?" he asked.

"What do you mean?"

"I mean, what are you doing today?"

"Nothing. Errands. Chores."

"Can you wait here for an hour?"

"Why?"

"I want to take you to Phoenix House."

Oh. I nodded.

"Good. Stay here." He lifted an admonishing finger.

Detective Peters grunted his way onto the landing. "I should have figured you'd be here."

"Give her a break, Peters. This looks domestic. No way she had anything to do with it." Anarchy was defending me.

"Two murders and an attempted in less than a week, and she's been around for all of them."

It was hard to argue with Detective Peters' logic.

I didn't try. Besides, Anarchy was on my side. Who cared what Detective Peters thought?

"Let's do the walk through." Anarchy jerked his head toward the door.

Peters merely grunted.

Together they entered Karen's apartment.

"She let him in. Door's intact," said Peters.

I edged away from my assigned spot near the window, closer to the bannister, where I had a view inside Karen's apartment.

"They fought. Someone got hit with a lamp." Peters was just full of insights.

I'd seen the blood on the lamp shards; it wasn't as if he was blazing new territory.

"At some point, she ran for the kitchen," said Anarchy.

"Why? You think she wanted a knife?"

She'd wanted the phone and her attacker had ripped it from the wall.

"Phone." Anarchy had reached the same conclusion I had. "We ought to look at the ex-husband."

"Oh? Why?"

"Mrs. Russell says they had a nasty divorce."

Detective Peters shifted his gaze from the ruins in the living room to the hallway where I stood. "Does she?" He kicked at the door and it slammed with a *bang*.

A first. I'd never actually had a door slammed in my face before. I didn't much like it.

"He's very grumpy, isn't he?" Joanne Graham, the woman who'd inadvertently started all the trouble between me and Anarchy, stood in her doorway.

"Yes."

"Would you like coffee? You look as if you could use a cup."

I dredged up a smile. "That's very kind of you. Thank you."

"Come on in."

*When one door closes, another door opens.*

Joanne Graham's apartment was similar to Karen's—except for the destroyed part. That and the furnishings. Karen's place looked as if it was populated with things she'd won in her divorce settlement. A mish-mash. Joanne's place managed hip and cozy at the same time—papasan chairs with red cushions, leather poufs, and a glass and brass coffee table.

"Let me take your coat." She held out her hands.

I'd been glad of my coat in the chilly hallway. Here in Joanne's warm apartment, I didn't need it. I took it off and handed it to her.

She folded it over her arm and disappeared into what was presumably the bedroom.

"Have you lived here long?" I asked when she returned.

"Two years." She led me to a tiny kitchen where Mr. Coffee's identical twin waited to make all things right with the world.

"How well did you know Karen, Miss Graham?"

"Please call me Joanne."

"Thank you, I'm Ellison."

She smiled and added water and grounds to Mr. Coffee. "I knew Karen to say hello to. She was quiet when she first moved in. It's only recently that she's started coming out of her shell."

"Oh?"

"This guy on the third floor had a Halloween party for all the tenants. Karen and I chatted and I warned her about John Hasty."

"John Hasty?"

"The building Lothario. He hits on every woman he sees."

"And he hit on Karen?"

Joanne nodded and took two mugs down from the cabinet. "Cream and sugar?"

"Just cream." I liked Joanne Graham. A lot. "Did Karen go out with him?"

"You know—" Joanne tilted her head "—I think she did." She shuddered. "The women in the building call him *Hands*. He asked her and she said yes before I had a chance to warn her." She reached into a small refrigerator and paused, her hand hovering above the cream. "You know, I think they went out last night."

We pondered that for a few seconds.

The hand holding the cream shook. "You don't think he—"

"That he got angry when she kept his hands at arm's length?"

"Exactly."

There'd been so much anger. Surely too much for one date. "No. Of course not." But maybe Karen going out on a date had made Daniel mad enough to beat her. "You should tell the police what you just told me."

"It would be no hardship to spend some time with the tall one."

I liked her less. A lot less.

We took our coffee to the living room and chatted—about

living on the Plaza, about Mr. Coffee's many stellar qualities, and about her cat, Felix, who wandered in from the bedroom.

"Ellison?" Anarchy's voice was audible through the door.

"There's the tall one now." I stood. "Do you mind if I let him in?"

Joanne smoothed her hair and pinched some color into her cheeks. "Please do."

I opened the door to Joanne's apartment. "In here."

"I asked you not to move."

True, but Peters had kicked a door shut in my face and the gray light that filtered in through the window on the landing was beyond depressing. I shrugged and offered him an apologetic smile. "Joanne made coffee. I bet she has another mug." Who could refuse such an offer?

Anarchy Jones, that's who. "We have someplace to be. Get your coat."

I glanced over my shoulder at Joanne (I swear she put on lipstick in the few seconds my back was turned to her). "You should come in, if only for a moment." I opened the door wider and waited for Anarchy to cross the threshold. "Joanne, would you please tell Detective Jones what you told me about Hands?"

"Of course," she purred like Felix. A nice, attractive (very attractive) woman with good taste and a pleasant cat, and suddenly I couldn't stand her.

"I'll grab my coat." We would not be lingering in Joanne's apartment.

"Coffee, Detective Jones?" she asked.

"No, thank you."

*Whew.* I grabbed my coat from her bed and hurried back to the living room.

Anarchy wore his cop face and had a small notepad in hand. He looked impervious to Joanne's charms—maybe she wasn't so bad after all.

"John Hasty?" He jotted the name down. "Anything else?"

"No. That's all."

"Thank you, Miss Graham." He shifted his gaze to me. "Are you ready?"

"Yes. Thank you for the coffee, Joanne."

"You're welcome. Come back anytime." Why did I get the feeling she was talking to Anarchy and not me?

Anarchy and I descended five flights of stairs and stepped outside into the cold.

I shivered. "*Brrr.*"

"I'll turn the heat up." He took my arm and led me to his car.

"But—"

"Your car will be fine where it is, Ellison. Just get in."

I didn't argue.

Anarchy drove me to a neighborhood I didn't know existed, pulled into a gated driveway, and pushed an intercom button. "Detective Anarchy Jones. Purple Rabbit."

The gate swung open.

"Purple rabbit?" I asked.

"It's this week's password."

"Password?"

"The location is a secret and they change the password every week."

"Oh."

The driveway wound through trees that hid the house. "The entire place is surrounded by a six-foot wall topped with broken glass and razor wire."

"Oh."

He reached across the front seat, claimed my hand, and squeezed. "It's here to keep the women safe."

I nodded, unable to find words other than *oh*.

Anarchy parked in front of a rambling older home with big eaves and what looked like a steel front door. He put the car in park. "The driveway is slick. Wait until I can help you."

"I'll be fine." I closed my fingers around the door handle.

"Ellison, just wait."

I waited.

Anarchy circled the car, opened my door, and helped me out. Together we negotiated the icy front steps and waited for someone to open the front door.

"This is Phoenix House?"

He nodded.

The door opened and a young woman—not more than five or six years older than Grace—waved us inside. "Come in, it's cold out there." She regarded me with kind eyes. "I'm Gloria."

"Nice to meet you, Gloria." I extended my hand. "I'm Ellison Russell."

She shook my hand and turned her attention to Anarchy. "We haven't seen much of you lately, Detective Jones."

"I'm working homicide," he said.

"Women we couldn't help." Gloria's voice which had been bright and welcoming now sounded as gray as the weather outside. Her gaze swung back to me. "Were you able to bring anything with you?"

I glanced down at the handbag hanging from my arm.

"It's not what you think, Gloria," said Anarchy. "Mrs. Russell and Khaki White were friends." That was overstating things a bit. And what exactly did Gloria think?

Tears filled Gloria's brown eyes. "I didn't realize. Khaki was an angel. I don't know what we're going to do without her."

"Would you please give Mrs. Russell a tour?"

"Of course," said Gloria. "Come this way."

She led us into the living room where two small girls held looper looms on their laps. A mound of colorful loom loopers lay between them. Each girl held a red plastic hook.

"I get the purples," said the blonde child.

"Fine, but I get the greens. Mommy wants a green kitchen."

They were making potholders.

Their mother, whose left eye sported shades of both purple and green, smiled down at them.

"Phoenix House can accommodate up to ten women and their children," said Gloria.

I swallowed. Really, I needed to come up with something better than *oh*. "Oh?"

"We're at capacity right now."

Ten women hiding from their husbands? I looked more closely at the woman on the couch. She wore bell-bottom jeans and a loose sweater. She looked like someone I would fail to notice on a busy sidewalk.

"How do the women who come here find you?" There. I'd managed something other than *oh*.

"The police bring them here. They usually arrive with nothing."

And she'd asked me if I brought anything with me...I blinked. Did I look like someone whose husband hit her?

Gloria was still talking. "We give them clothes, underwear, and toiletries. More important we give them a safe place and counseling."

"Counseling?"

Gloria kept her voice low, barely a whisper. "The women who come here have been in abusive relationships for years. They've come to believe the poison their partners have been feeding them. They're worthless. They only get hit because they've done something wrong. They're nothing."

We passed through the living room and into the dining room.

A woman with well-coiffed hair and a silk blouse sat at the head of the table and sipped from a coffee cup. I didn't know her, but I could have. She wouldn't have looked out of place at a bridge table at the club or at one of Mother's charity luncheons.

"Is that the executive director?" I asked.

"No. That's Mary. She's been staying with us for about six days."

"What?" I stared. Until this morning when I found Karen, it never occurred to me that someone I knew—someone who swam in my ocean—would be married to someone who hit her.

"Did you think wealth or privilege excluded a woman from violence?" Gloria sounded almost amused.

I'd thought exactly that. My footing, which had always seemed so suré, swayed beneath me.

Anarchy wrapped my hand in his. Big, safe, reassuring.

"I—" I shook my head. Even at his worst, when he was doing his damnedest to undermine my confidence as an artist, Henry never hit me. "I had no idea." I manufactured a smile for Mary who was looking at me with an empathetic tilt to her head. "How did Khaki get involved here?"

"She had a friend whose husband abused her."

Who? I didn't ask. Whoever Khaki's friend was, she deserved privacy.

"I believe it was a friend from college," Gloria added. "She died."

"How awful."

"Khaki realized that abuse wasn't limited to working class families. She did her best to get women—" she didn't add *like you* "—out of potentially dangerous situations."

We finished the tour, me mute except for the occasional *oh*. We ended up at the front door.

"Thanks, Gloria," said Anarchy.

"Wait." I dug a checkbook and a pen out of my handbag. I'd given Cora thousands of dollars to bring Phyllis Schlafly to town. The least I could do was triple that amount for a place that actually helped women. I signed the check and handed it to Gloria.

Her eyes widened. "Thank you."

"You're welcome." I looked up at Anarchy whose brown eyes were a bit misty. "I'm ready."

He led me outside. "I didn't take you there so you'd make a donation."

"I know."

He opened the passenger door for me. "That was very generous of you."

I climbed into the car. Despite the cold, I felt warm. "I wish it could have been more."

It would be.

# NINETEEN

Anarchy drove with both hands on the wheel, his gaze locked on the slick road in front of us. "Are you hungry?"

How could I be hungry after all I'd seen? My stomach gurgled, surprising me with its emphatic answer. "Yes."

For a half-second he pulled his gaze from the road and looked at me. "We're not far from my favorite place for fried chicken."

I hadn't eaten anything fried since early 1972, but fried chicken—especially fried chicken at Anarchy's favorite restaurant—sounded delicious. "Perfect."

He parked beneath a bridge (zero white Mercedes) and led me into a ramshackle building perched on the edge of a river bank. The floor sloped toward the river, and I imagined I could feel the whole building sliding toward the water.

I glanced at Anarchy and he gave me a reassuring smile. "It's hung on this long. I bet we're safe for the afternoon."

I was willing to trust him.

A denim-clad hostess led us to a table and handed us menus.

"Don't even think about ordering a salad." Anarchy peeked at me over the top of his menu. The expression in his eyes warmed me all the way to my cold toes. "You've had a rough day. You deserve a decent meal. In fact—" he reached across the table and plucked the menu from my fingers "—I'm ordering for both of us."

A waiter approached the table. "May I—"

"Two beers." Anarchy's twinkling gaze remained locked to mine. "Bud. Draft if you've got it."

"I don't drink beer."

"Try it. You might like it. Besides, it won't hurt you to learn how the other half lives."

My tongue tied itself into knots. Double knots.

He leaned forward, resting his arms on the table. "Are you all right?"

I'd be better if my heart would stop running wind sprints.

The space between his brows furrowed and he rested his chin on his hand. "First Karen Fleming, then Phoenix House. It's a lot for one day."

I couldn't talk. And not because of Karen or Phoenix House. This was Anarchy as I seldom saw him—relaxed, at ease. I nodded.

The waiter reappeared and put two beers on the table.

I lifted the heavy glass mug and gulped.

Anarchy watched me. His eyes, which had been looking very cop-like of late, were warm. He shifted his attention to the waiter. "We'll both have chicken dinners. Green beans. Mashed potatoes."

The young man made a note on his pad and scurried away.

I sipped again. Somehow, the beer untangled the knots in my tongue. "Drinking on duty, Detective Jones?"

Anarchy lifted his mug. "I'm not on duty, Mrs. Russell. This is my weekend off."

"But—"

"I came because you called."

An internal cartwheel (he came because I called!) slammed face first into guilt. "I ruined your Saturday. I'm sorry. Did you have anything planned?"

He looked down at his beer. "Stanford's playing USC."

Whatever that meant.

"I ruined Detective Peters' Saturday too. No wonder he's so cranky."

"He's always cranky." Anarchy lifted his mug to his lips.

"Why?"

"Same old. Peters is an old school cop. I went to college. I'm not exactly his dream partner."

That seemed a ridiculous reason to be cranky. I said as much.

"Cut him some slack. He's third-generation cop. He's not big on change." Anarchy stared across the table into my eyes.

I smoothed the gingham napkin on my lap. What exactly was Anarchy saying? That I wasn't big on change either?

The sound of coins hitting the floor saved me from commenting. The coins rolled across the tilted floor like marbles in a chute. A lone quarter finished its journey near our table. We both watched it spin and fall.

The silence that followed was itchy.

Anarchy bent, picked up the coin, and handed it to the little boy who'd dropped it.

"Thank you, sir." The child took off in search of the rest of his fallen money.

I cast about for a new topic. "Do you think Daniel Fleming is the one who did that to Karen?" I didn't expect an answer. It was an open case. Anarchy never commented on open cases.

He surprised me and said, "That much rage? It's usually domestic."

"Is that why you took me to Phoenix House?"

"I took you to Phoenix House to convince you that some of the men you know are capable of violence."

Seeing Karen had convinced me of that.

"They're not picky about who they hit, Ellison. If you've been asking questions about domestic violence, you need to stop."

I hadn't been asking questions. Not even one. An image of Karen's battered face flitted across the back of my eyelids. Maybe I *should've* been asking questions. "I never imagined someone I knew would have a husband who hit her."

"You're not alone." The expression in Anarchy's eyes shifted from warm and melty to serious. "Let me do my job. I'll catch Khaki's killer, and Stan's, and the man who beat Karen. I don't want you involved in any way."

I took another sip of beer. "About Khaki."

He crossed his arms over his chest and his expression turned even more serious.

I wanted the smiling, easy-going Anarchy back. "I just want to tell you one thing."

He relaxed. Marginally.

"There's something off. She charged ridiculous amounts of money for antiques."

"And her clients didn't complain?"

How to explain? "There's a certain mindset that paying the most means you get the best. If anyone complained, it was simply a way to highlight they could afford to pay her prices." Thornton's complaints about the kitchen table came to mind. "Hiring Khaki became something of a status symbol."

"So what's the problem?"

"The number of couples who got divorced after she finished with their houses." Another sip. Beer wasn't so bad. "She did Karen and Daniel's house."

"Are you saying Khaki White had affairs with her clients' husbands?"

"No." I was making a complete hash of this explanation. "I don't know what she did."

"Is that all?" The smile was back, and it was most distracting.

Khaki's high fees and the divorce rate among her clients sounded so unimportant now that I'd told him. In my head, those facts had been epic. "I suppose so."

"Thank you for telling me." When Anarchy smiled, the skin around his eyes crinkled. Crinkled in a way that made my own lips curl.

"Two chicken dinners." The waiter put down two platters—platters not plates—of food.

I gaped at the trough in front of me. "I'll never be able to eat all this."

Anarchy grinned. Grinned and my heart skipped a beat. "Try."

When we'd devoured all that was humanly possible (I collected a ridiculously large doggie bag for Max), Anarchy drove me back to my car.

"I'll follow you home."

"There's no need." The freezing rain had stopped and the streets were wet rather than slick.

"I want to see you safely home."

There it was—my heart doing another sprint. "Thank you."

I drove home listening to Carol King sing about a man who could take her to paradise and bring her to her knees. I sang with her, hyper-aware that the headlights in my rearview mirror belonged to Anarchy.

He followed me into the driveway, parked behind me, and was at my car door before I had time to collect my purse and the doggie bag from the passenger's seat.

My blood fizzed and the smile that rose to my lips was involuntary, appearing of its own volition.

"I'll see you to the door." He held out his hand and I took it. Electricity zinged past the protective leather of our gloves.

The late afternoon light was fading and the front stoop was cast in shadow. I searched my purse for a house key.

"Ellison."

I looked up.

Anarchy caught my chin between his thumb and fingers.

My tongue went back to being tied in knots.

Despite the cold air, I was suddenly burning up.

He drew me closer and his lips touched mine.

I groaned. I melted. I forgot all about standing on my own, finding myself, and being a woman who roared.

His other hand caressed the nape of my neck.

Our lips parted.

His tongue—

Inside the house, Max barked. The front light flipped on, and I jumped away from Anarchy quicker than Rosie ever dreamed of wiping up spills with Bounty.

Anarchy caught my wrist. "Wait."

Someone was going to open that door and catch us.

"Will you go out with me again?"

Is that what we'd done? Gone out? On a date?

What I'd told Hunter played through my mind. *I need to find out what it's like to be on my own before I can be with anyone.* But instead of repeating that, I said, "Yes."

The door opened and Grace peered out. "You're home."

Guilty as charged. "I am."

"Granna's been trying to get in touch with you all afternoon. She wants you to call her right away."

I swallowed a sigh. "Thanks for seeing me home, Anarchy."

"My pleasure." His eyes twinkled. "I'll call you."

I ignored the speculative look on Grace's face. "Good night."

"Good night."

No one moved.

We stood there in the cold until Grace rolled her eyes. "Granna's waiting."

With one last, lingering look at the man I had no business wanting, I trudged into the house where Max nudged the doggie bag with his nose.

It was Grace who closed the door on Anarchy.

"What does your grandmother want?"

"I don't know, but she sounded upset."

"Where's Aunt Sis?"

"She was able to get a flight back to Akron. She told me to tell you thank you and she'll call you later in the week."

I carried the leftovers into the kitchen and put them on the counter.

"Where did you eat?" asked Grace.

"A fried chicken place."

"You ate fried food?" Grace's tone was disbelieving.

"I did."

"You like him." Her voice held a hint of accusation. "I *knew* you liked him."

"What if I do?"

That stopped her. She thought a moment. "You seem happier when you're with him, so I guess I like him too. Granna, on the other hand..."

She didn't need to finish her sentence. I knew exactly how Mother would feel about my seeing Anarchy.

"No idea what your granna wants?"

"None." Grace pulled the bag of leftovers closer. "Is there chicken in here?"

"Yes."

Max donned a worried expression.

I picked up the phone and dialed.

Mother's housekeeper answered on the second ring. "Hello."

"Penelope, this is Ellison. I'm returning Mother's call."

"Good evening, Miss Ellison. Your mother asked me to tell you that she needs you at the hospital. Your cousin Cora fell down the stairs."

Oh dear Lord. Poor Cora, she was having a horrible week. "Is she all right?"

"She's at the hospital, Miss Ellison."

Yes, but there was a difference between a broken leg and a broken neck. "Thank you, Penelope." I hung up the phone and turned to Grace who was nibbling on a chicken breast under Max's unwavering gaze. "I've got to go to the hospital. Cora had an accident."

Grace, her mouth full of fried chicken, merely nodded.

"I don't know when I'll be home."

She nodded again.

"Give some of that to Max."

Max favored me with a grateful glance.


The woman sitting behind the information desk at the hospital was vaguely familiar. "Good evening, Mrs. Russell." Did everyone at the hospital know my name?

"Good evening. I'm looking for my cousin, Mrs. Thornton Knight."

She studied a list of names. "Cora Knight? Three-fourteen."

"Thank you. What about Karen Fleming?"

The woman consulted her list. "She's in intensive care."

Poor Karen.

"And Jinx George?"

Another consultation. "She's in room—"

"Thank you." I already knew Jinx's room number. The question was to ascertain if she was still there.

I trudged to the elevator and pushed the up button.

"Hold the eleva—oh, it's you. Your mother will be glad you're here." My father, who held two steaming paper cups, leaned forward and kissed my cheek. The scent of coffee filled the air around us.

"What happened to Cora, Daddy?"

"She tripped."

"And?"

"Her collar bone is broken and she has a possible head injury. She's still unconscious."

The elevator arrived and we climbed aboard.

"Thornton found her." Daddy shook his head. "He's beside himself."

I pushed the button for the third floor. "How long have you been here?"

"Since two."

The elevator began its glacially slow climb.

"Daddy?"

"Yes?"

"Is the Stanford USC game a big deal?"

He cocked his head to the side. I didn't usually ask questions about football. I *never* asked questions about football. "Yes, Ellison. For alumni, it's a very big deal."

The elevator doors slid open and we stepped into the hallway. Despite the hospital smell, despite the fact that my cousin's wife lay in a hospital bed, despite the very real possibility that Mother would spend the next three hours scolding me, my heart sang. Anarchy Jones had skipped watching a big game to spend the afternoon with me.

We walked halfway down an antiseptic hallway and entered Cora's room.

"There you are." It was the Frances Walford equivalent of *where the hell have you been?*

Daddy handed her a cup of coffee. He gave the other to Thornton.

Mother took a tiny sip. "This is awful."

Daddy shrugged, immune to her bad mood. "They made it fresh for you, Frannie."

Thornton sipped and grimaced.

"You've been here all afternoon?" I asked.

"Yes. And I'd like to know where—"

"You must be hungry." If I let Mother get a head of steam, there would be no stopping the diatribe. "I'll sit with Cora. Why don't you go get something to eat?"

"I couldn't ask you to do that." Thornton shook his head.

"Don't be silly. We're family. Run on over to Winstead's and get yourselves hamburgers and decent cups of coffee."

"She's right, Thornton." It was hardly surprising Daddy agreed with my plan. Six o'clock was dinner time.

Mother stood and disappeared into the bathroom. The sound of coffee being poured down the sink was unmistakable. She reappeared. "Let's go, Thornton. We won't be gone long, and there's no sense in all of us just sitting around."

"What if she wakes up and I'm not here?" Thornton was being far more solicitous of unconscious Cora than he ever was when she was alert.

"I'll tell her you'll be back in a jiffy. Go. You'll feel better after you eat."

They went.

I settled into the chair nearest Cora's bed and picked up the paper. A judge had dismissed the charges against the guardsmen who fired on the students at Kent State.

"Ellison?"

I dropped the newspaper to the floor and leaned forward.

"Cora! How are you feeling?"

"May I have some water?"

A cup with a bendy straw sat on the table next to her bed. I held the straw to her lips and she drank.

When she'd had enough she turned her head. "He's not here?"

"Thornton? He's been here all afternoon. He left just a few minutes ago with Mother and Daddy. They went to Winstead's for something to eat. He'll be back soon."

The noise Cora made sounded an awful lot like a whimper.

The blood in my veins formed ice crystals. I'd already seen one woman whose husband hurt her. "Cora, did Thornton do this to you?"

"No!" Cora winced as if speaking emphatically made her head hurt. "How could you suggest such a thing?"

Because I'd seen Karen. Because I'd been to Phoenix House. "If he did, we can get you help."

She turned her head away. "I don't need any help." Never had I heard anyone sound so bleak.

"Cora—" she didn't respond to her name "—I'll help you."

"I don't need help." She spoke to the wall, not me.

"Cora." I instilled her name with empathy.

"I tripped." The wall remained more interesting than anything I might say.

"On what?"

A few seconds passed. "My own feet."

I didn't believe her. "Why are you covering for him?"

"It was my fault. The luncheon was a disaster and that's on me."

"What does that have to do with your tripping?"

"Go. Away."

"No. You need help, Cora. Tell me what happened."

"He'll kill me." I'd heard that so often. *When Preston gets the Harzfeld's bill, he'll kill me.* Said it so often. *Mother will kill me if I'm late subbing at her bridge game.* This was the first time I'd heard *he'll kill me* and knew the person speaking meant it. Literally.

"We're going to get you help."

"Don't get involved, Ellison." Cora's voice was thick with tears. She turned her head and her eyes were red-rimmed and her nose was scarlet. "Look what happened to the last person who tried to help me."

Oh dear Lord. She didn't mean...

"Look what happened to Khaki."

# TWENTY

I collapsed onto the uncomfortable hospital chair (so many naugas sacrificed for no good reason), ignored the rude sound it made, and gaped at Cora. "Thornton killed Khaki?"

Tears leaked from Cora's eyes.

What was I going to tell Mother? She adored Thornton. Adored him. And what about Anarchy? Yes, I'd identified Khaki's killer, but I'd done it within two hours of promising not to get involved.

What about poor Stan? Had Thornton killed him in my house with fifty people around? I dropped my head to my hands.

"You don't believe me." Her face crumpled. "You're on his side."

"No." I reached out and took Cora's hand. "I'm on yours."

"I'm so tired of feeling frightened all the time. Every day I wait for the sky to fall."

I squeezed her hand. "We'll get you someplace safe, and we'll get you a lawyer."

The door to Cora's room pushed open and we stiffened as if we'd been caught doing something wrong.

A nurse entered and smiled brightly. "We're awake. How are we feeling?"

"My head hurts." Cora's voice was faint.

"I'll page the doctor and ask if we can give you some meds for the pain."

The nurse picked up the chart hanging at the end of the bed and shifted her gaze to me. "How long has she been conscious?"

"Ten minutes."

She made a note.

"Cora is thirsty. May she please have some ice water?" The cup at the side of the bed was half-empty and tepid at best.

"Of course."

"Is there a telephone directory in here?"

The nurse pointed to the drawer of the bedside table.

"Thank you."

She bustled over to the bedside, took Cora's pulse, and laid her hand on Cora's forehead. More notes went on the chart. "I'll go get you that water."

She departed. I pulled open the drawer and plunked the phone book into my lap.

"Who are you calling?" asked Cora.

"Sally Broome." I ran my finger down the list of names. How was is that the print got smaller every year? I squinted and tapped. "There she is." I dialed.

"You won't reach her on a Saturday night."

True—but I couldn't phone the lawyer who would take my call on weekends. I'd told him I wanted to stand on my own; I could hardly ask for his help four days later. "I'll leave a message."

A disinterested voice answered the phone. "Answering service."

"This is Ellison Russell calling. Would you please have Ms. Broome call me?" I left my number.

Cora still looked worried.

"They'll keep you here for several days. You'll have Sally on retainer before you leave."

"Retainer?"

"A deposit to pay for her services."

"I don't have any money." The admission came with fresh tears.

"I do."

"Cora! You're awake." Mother spoke from the doorway. "You had us all so worried." With a few words Mother made it clear that Cora had caused everyone (or at least Mother) an immense amount of inconvenience. How would Mother feel when she learned that Cora hadn't tripped, that Thornton was a wife-beater and a murderer?

The man himself followed Mother into the room, hurried to Cora's bed, and dropped a kiss on her cheek. "Thank God you're awake."

Max once cornered a rabbit in the backyard. The poor little thing froze, its fear apparent only through its suddenly too big eyes. That was how Cora looked now. Frozen. Terrified.

I stood, drew a huge breath deep into my lungs, and planted my hands on my hips. "Thornton, we need to—"

Cora squeaked.

I glanced down at the bed.

She shook her head. More tears streamed down her cheeks. "No."

Had she lost her mind? The man had tried to kill her.

Cora seemed to shrink before my eyes, a tiny, too-thin woman in an enormous hospital bed. "I...I need to fight my own battles." Her left hand bunched the sheets, but she lifted her chin defiantly and stared at her husband. "I told Ellison what happened."

"What happened?" Mother's gaze traveled from Thornton to Cora and back again.

Thornton's shoulders slumped. "It's my fault."

I stared at him. He was admitting to attempted murder? Would he admit to killing Khaki next?

"Cora tripped." Mother held onto the truth as she knew it.

"No." Thornton shook his head. "Cora and I were having an argument at the top of the stairs. I jerked her arm and she fell."

Mother's face looked as if it had been hewn from Carrara marble. That pale. That hard. "Move out of the way, Ellison. I need to sit."

I ceded the uncomfortable chair to Mother. She sank. No rude sounds ensued. The naugas didn't dare.

Mother sat rigid, her back poker straight. With her crimson blouse and black skirt, she looked like the Red Queen. Next she'd look at me, the bearer of bad news, and declare *off with her head*.

I readied myself for a battle *royale*.

But Mother directed her ire at Thornton. "If you had her arm, how did she fall all the way down the stairs?"

"I lost my grip."

"Really?" With one word she demolished any argument he had or ever would have. "You told us she tripped." Mother's lip curled. "This is terribly déclassé."

Thornton's stolid expression didn't change. That Mother had just called him trashy hadn't registered. Yet.

The nurse pushed through the door with a pitcher in her hands and Daddy at her heels. "I brought water."

Given the icy fury emanating from Mother, the water in the pitcher probably froze solid as soon as she crossed the threshold.

The nurse put the pitcher down on the table, rubbed her arms for warmth, and backed out of the room. "I'll let you visit."

Too bad I couldn't escape with her.

"Thornton and Cora had an argument." Mother directed her remarks to Daddy. "He's responsible for her injuries."

"But you told the doctors she tripped." Sometimes Daddy was too sweet and kind for his own good. He failed to see the dark side in people.

"We are not that sort of family." Mother glared at Thornton. "Men in this family cherish their wives."

I snorted. Henry had not cherished me any more than Thornton, who'd spent the past several decades berating and belittling his wife, cherished Cora.

"This is not a family where men go down to—" Mother's chest puffed with righteous indignation "—gin joints, drink too much, then slap their wives around."

"I didn't hit Cora. It was an accident."

"Was it?" Mother was as angry as I'd ever seen her. "You had a fight at the top of a flight of stairs. You raised your hand to your wife and she fell. In my book, that doesn't sound like an accident. You pushed her down the stairs."

What had he done to Khaki and Stan White? An active grenade would make less of an impression than me accusing my cousin of murder. Frankly, I didn't think my family could handle the explosion. I bit my tongue.

On the other hand, Thornton was family. Did he deserve the right to defend himself before I told Anarchy?

The nurse made the decision for me. She came back with a doctor who kicked us all out of Cora's room. Even Mother. Apparently a medical degree made one brave.

While I might have accused Thornton of murder in private, I wasn't about to do it in a public hallway. Mother would never believe me. Not unless Thornton confessed. Since that seemed about as likely as Nixon regaining office, I marched up to the nursing station. "Mrs. Knight has just informed us that she didn't trip and fall. She was pushed." I cast a telling glance in her husband's direction. "Would you make certain she's not left alone?"

"Yes, ma'am."

"Mother, I'm exhausted. I'm going home."

She was so angry with Thornton for behaving like a low-rent, gin-guzzling, wife-beater, she didn't care what I did.

Thornton did. He followed me to the elevator. "Ellison, wait." His hand closed around my upper arm.

We both paused and looked at the pale skin on the back of his hand. The contrast with the fabric of my coat was marked.

"Take your hand off of me."

His grip tightened. "What did Cora tell you?"

"She didn't trip."

"What else?" He shook my arm hard enough to rattle my teeth.

I hated bullies. "Did you do it?" I asked. "Did you kill Khaki?"

"What the *hell* is going on?" Mother's gaze was fixed on my arm.

"Nothing." Thornton released me, pulled at the lapels of his jacket, then leveled a murderous glare my way. "I did not kill her."

I did not believe him.

I drove home. Somehow. My mind remained back at the hospital. Had Thornton killed Khaki and Stan? Why? Because they knew he was beating Cora? Because they'd tried to help her?

I sat in the driveway resting my head against the steering wheel until the cold drove me indoors.

Max met me at the front door. He watched as I pulled off my boots, a disgruntled expression on his doggy face. Had Grace forgotten to feed him?

And where exactly was Grace?

She was grounded. God help her if she'd gone out with her friends. The downstairs was quiet. She'd better be pouting in her room

"Are you hungry?" I asked Max.

He trotted toward the kitchen and dinner.

I padded after him. The light over the kitchen sink was on and the counters were spotless.

Now that Max was in the kitchen, he ignored the door that hid his kibble. Instead he sat next to the entrance to the darkened family room and stared at me. So he wasn't hungry.

I went to the refrigerator and paused, my hand on the door. Wine or scotch?

Scotch. I'd definitely had the kind of day that required a neat scotch, a hot bath, and a good night's sleep.

There was scotch in the family room. I let go of the refrigerator handle and joined Max at the entrance.

The television was on and David Carradine flickered across the screen. Grace must have been gone for a while. There was no way she'd purposefully tune in to *Kung Fu*.

I flipped on the light.

Two teenagers levitated off the couch. If I'd zapped them both with cattle prods the reaction wouldn't have been any greater. Their flight into the ether was accompanied by a strangled cry, "Moooooom."

I stood unmoving, my feet unable to shift so much as an inch. In the brief instant Grace hovered above the couch, I'd noticed her shirt was unbuttoned.

The other teenager was a boy.

Merciful God, the day I'd had and now this. "I will give you one minute to get yourselves straightened around."

I returned to the kitchen and pressed one burning cheek and then the other against the cool glass of the back door. What was Grace thinking?

Max gave me an I-tried-to-tell-you look.

The seconds ticked by on the kitchen clock.

With heavy feet, I returned to the family room.

Trip Michaels stood next to the couch where Grace sat with her head in her hands.

"Trip, how did you get here?" There'd been no car in the drive.

"A friend dropped me off."

"Then I suggest you call someone for a ride."

He pulled at the collar of his sweater and swallowed. "I can walk home. It's only a few blocks."

"I'll see you to the door." If Henry were alive, he'd threaten Trip with castration. Somehow I doubted the threat would be as credible coming from me. This was one of those rare occasions I missed Henry. I paused with my hand on the door knob. "You know, Trip, your grandmother and Grace's grandmother play bridge every week."

"Oh?" He slipped into his coat and kept his gaze on the floor.

"Yes. And your father and my sister, Marjorie, graduated from high school together."

"Really?"

"Your mother and I have worked on so many of the same committees together I've lost count."

He looked up. "What are you saying, Mrs. Russell?"

"I'm saying that our two families have been friends for generations. Don't screw it up."

"No, ma'am." He scurried out the front door without a backward glance.

I returned to the family room and Grace. "You know the rules. No boys without an adult in the house."

"I'm an adult."

"You are sixteen. Yesterday you got arrested. Today I find you half-naked with a boy on our family room couch."

She crossed her arms. "You make me sound like some kind of delinquent."

"Not at all. I'm just questioning your choices."

"I don't want to talk about it."

That made two of us.

"Teenage boys are walking hormones."

"Oh. Ugh, Mom. No. We are not talking about this."

"Yes, we are. Trip isn't some boy you've been dating for months. One who cares about you. He broke up with Dawn what's-her-name earlier this week."

"You just don't understand. Things are different now."

Maybe she was right. I came of age before the sexual revolution. But some things hadn't changed. "All girls—all women—deserve someone who treats them with respect."

"He respects me."

*That's why he was feeling you up on a couch?* I stopped myself before I said it. Thank God. "Be that as it may—"

"Are you forbidding me to see him?" A mulish expression settled onto her face.

That would make him utterly irresistible. "No. I'm asking you to take things slow. Get past his hormones." And yours.

She wanted to argue—she stood, planted her hands on her hips, and jutted her chin forward—but I hadn't given her anything to argue about. She went with an old stand-by and rolled her eyes. "I'm going to bed."

It was eight thirty. I didn't argue.

Turned out, finding one's daughter making out in the dark sapped the last bit of energy one possessed. Cora and Thornton and Khaki and Stan would have to wait. I couldn't deal with one more thing.

# TWENTY-ONE

*Brnggg, brnng.*

My hand snaked out from under the covers and grabbed the phone. "Hello." Somehow I pronounced the word as one syllable. *Hell.*

"Mrs. Russell?"

"Speaking." Or trying to.

"This is Sally Broome calling. Did I wake you?"

Sally Broome. Sally Broome? My sleep-fuddled brain searched for why I knew Sally Broome.

Lawyer. Cora.

I cracked an eye and peered at the clock on my bedside table. Eight thirty. On a Sunday morning. "No. Of course I'm up." I propped myself up and rubbed my eyes with my free hand.

"It is early." She sounded apologetic.

"Not at all." After the week I'd had, sleeping till nine on a Sunday seemed entirely reasonable. "I've been up for hours."

"I'm returning your call."

Lawyer. Cora. "Right. I'm calling on behalf of my cousin."

A few seconds ticked by. I watched each one pass on the clock next to my bed.

"I prefer for my clients to call me themselves."

"My cousin is in the hospital, Ms. Broome."

"Oh?" A politely interested *oh.*

"She was pushed down a flight of stairs."

"Oh." A call-to-action *oh.*

"She would like to retain your services."

"I see. Who is your cousin?"

"Cora Knight."

More seconds ticked by on the clock. Fifteen of them. Fifteen seconds that lasted an eternity.

"Ms. Broome, are you there?"

"Yes. Sorry. Correct me if I'm wrong, but isn't it Mr. Knight who's your cousin?"

"He is."

"And you want to retain me to represent his wife?"

"I do."

"Did Mr. Knight put Mrs. Knight in the hospital?"

"He did."

"I'd like to speak with you in person before I take the case."

"Are you free for brunch?" She'd probably had nine o'clock Tuesday morning in mind. But I'd already issued the invitation. I couldn't retract it now.

"Fine. Where?"

She wanted me to make decisions before coffee? "My country club at ten."

It was only after I'd given her the address and hung up the phone that I considered what a poor place I'd chosen for our meeting. We'd be the talk of the dining room. After all, what could a widow want with a divorce attorney?

I threw off the covers and stumbled downstairs for a confab with Mr. Coffee. I needed what only he could give me before I made any more terrible decisions.

I pushed Mr. Coffee's button and he went to work. Max scratched on the back door and I let him out in the backyard. The last of the leaves had fallen and hardy mums on the patio weren't looking so hardy. Winter had arrived.

Max, who liked the cold as much as I liked herbal tea, took care of his doggy business quickly, then trotted back inside, sat on his haunches, and waited for his treat.

I handed over a biscuit. "I'm tired of drama, Max."

He didn't care. He took his biscuit to his lair behind the kitchen table and ate it.

I sat at the kitchen counter, sipped coffee, and stared into space.

Had Thornton really killed two people? If so, why? No good reason came to mind. True, Khaki might have tried to help Cora escape her terrible marriage, but was that worth killing over? And why Stan?

Ugh. I buried my head in my arms.

Grace breezed past me without speaking.

I lifted my head. "Good morning."

"Hmph." She poured herself a cup of coffee, took a container of yogurt from the fridge and a spoon from the silverware drawer, and disappeared up the back stairs without saying a word.

The teenage silent treatment.

"You love me, don't you, Max?"

He stared at me with soulful eyes. He'd love me more if I gave him another biscuit.

I rubbed my forehead and drank deeply from my coffee cup. I had to tell Anarchy about Thornton. Had to.

And there was no time like the present. I poured myself another cup of coffee, picked up the phone, and dialed. The line rang and rang. I hung up and called the police department. "Hello, I'd like to speak with Detective Anarchy Jones."

"I'll put you through to the squad room, ma'am."

The line rang. Four rings. Five. Six. Seve—

"Hello." A man with enough gravel in his voice to pave a driveway spoke.

Double ugh. "Detective Peters?"

"Yeah."

"This is Ellison Russell calling. May I please speak with Detective Jones?"

"He's not here."

"May I leave a message?"

He grunted.

I took that as a yes. "Would you please have him call me at his earliest convenience?"

"Why?"

There was no way I was explaining my suspicions about a family member to Detective Peters. No way. "Please just have him call me."

He grunted and hung up the phone.

I topped off my coffee cup and went upstairs to prepare for brunch at the club. I showered, dried my hair and twisted it into a chignon, applied makeup, and donned one of my new outfits from Swanson's—a belted wool suit the color of bittersweet.

Ready, I paused outside Grace's door and tapped.

No answer.

"Grace, I'm going to brunch. I'll be back in a few hours."

No answer.

I sighed and descended the stairs.

The mink or the camel hair coat? I tarried, undecided.

*Brnng, brnng.*

Which coat?

*Brnng, brngg.*

I reached for the mink.

"Phone." Grace's voice carried all the way down the stairs. Whoever was on the other end of the phone line was probably now deaf in one ear.

I glanced at my watch and hurried to the kitchen extension. I was already cutting it close to arrive on time. "Hello."

"Hi."

Honey, warm and sweet, replaced the blood in my veins. No. No. No. There was no time to moon over the sound of Anarchy's voice. A woman who'd needed the address to the country club wouldn't feel comfortable waiting for me alone. Anarchy's timing was awful. "I'm on my way to brunch, but I think I may have found something."

"What?"

"I'm running terribly late. Can you come over around noon? I'll tell you everything."

"Ellison." His voice held a warning—his murder investigation was more important than anything I had planned.

Except in this one case it wasn't. Cora needed a lawyer. Right away. Before she got sent home with the man who'd put her in the hospital.

"Please, just come over at noon. I've got to go." I hung up the phone before he could change my mind, raced out the back door, hopped into my car, and sped to the club.

There were four white Mercedes in the parking lot.

I parked far away from all of them and hurried inside.

Sally Broome stood just inside the door. Like me, she wore a suit. Unlike me, hers was serviceable gray.

"I'm so sorry I'm late. The phone wouldn't stop ringing." I held out my hand and we shook.

"No need to apologize. I just arrived myself."

The hostess led us to the dining room and we sat. "A drink, Mrs. Russell?"

I nodded toward my guest. "Ms. Broome?"

"Coffee."

The idea of a Bloody Mary was alluring. The idea of explaining my theory about Thornton to Anarchy after I'd been drinking was not. "Two coffees, please."

"Yes, ma'am. The buffet is open."

"Thank you." I turned to Sally. "Sunday brunch is buffet. I hope you don't mind."

"Not at all. I'd like to ask you—"

"Ellison!" Jane Addison stood in front of us. She wore a winter white dress and a curious gleam in her sharp eyes.

"Good morning, Jane." I made no move to introduce her to Sally.

Jane was not deterred. She thrust out her hand. "Jane Addison."

"Sally Broome."

Jane already knew that. She wanted to know why a widow was brunching with a divorce attorney.

Jane held onto Sally's hand and pumped. "Pleased to meet you. How do you know Ellison?"

A waiter saved Sally from answering. He put coffee down in front of both of us.

Sally extracted her hand.

"Sally and I are old friends, Jane. We've got a lot of catching up to do." As hints went, it was not subtle. Then again, Jane Addison didn't respond to subtle.

"I need to join my husband." She nodded toward her long-suffering spouse. "But before I go, I must know—is Jinx still in the hospital?"

My stomach tightened with guilt. "I haven't spoken with her yet today."

I should have called.

"I've never known Jinx to be exhausted."

Was that what Preston was telling people? "Yes, well—" I raised my hand and waved at Jane's stolid spouse. He waved back. "Is your husband waving at you?"

Jane sighed. "So nice to meet you, Ms. Broome. Ellison, let's have coffee?"

"We'll do it soon," I lied.

Jane returned to her table where her food had grown cold.

"No one will bother us once we've filled our plates." Not *exactly* true. People were less likely to interrupt if one was eating, but a plate of eggs benedict couldn't keep the truly curious at bay.

We joined the buffet line. Mother's friend, Lorna Michaels, stood in front of us. Not just Mother's friend but also Trip's grandmother.

"Good morning, Lorna."

She responded with a regal nod. Lorna might not be so high and mighty if she knew what her grandson was up to. But since he was up to it with my daughter, silence was definitely golden.

"Good morning." Lorna eyed Sally over the top of her glasses. "Ellison, I don't believe I know your friend."

"Lorna, may I introduce Sally Broome. Sally, this is Lorna Michaels, a dear friend of the family."

The dear friend of the family narrowed her eyes.

Ellison at brunch with a divorce lawyer? Mother would know within the hour.

Sally and I returned to our table, smoothed napkins over our laps, and picked up our forks. "So tell me about your cousin," said Sally.

"Cora or Thornton?"

"Both."

Easier said than done. "Thornton has always been dismissive of Cora, but I never dreamed he—" I reached for my coffee. How had I been so blind? "—I never dreamed he'd hurt her physically."

"Why would you? Most women never dream such a thing could happen to someone they know."

"Khaki White did."

Sally's glance was diamond-edged sharp. "What do you know about Khaki White?"

"I know she was on the board at Phoenix House." And she was murdered in my study.

Sally's lips thinned to a tight line. "Khaki did everything she could to help women get out of dangerous situations."

The hand holding my coffee cup froze halfway to my mouth. "What did she do?"

"So many wives have nothing except what their husbands give them. It's hard for them to leave."

"And?"

"And Khaki decorated their houses."

I sipped and thought. And thought.

Sally didn't interrupt. Instead she picked at her omelet and watched the people watching us.

The fourth cup of coffee kicked my brain into gear. "She

overcharged men and gave the money to the wives who left them."

"I did not say that." Spoken like a lawyer.

That meant Daniel Fleming had paid for the antiques that bought his wife's freedom. That meant Thornton had done the same.

"Who else knew?"

"Who else knew what?" Sally wore a politely interested lawyer mask. She wasn't going to tell me.

"If Khaki was helping women get out of dangerous marriages, were any of the board members at Phoenix House aware of what she was doing?"

"I can neither confirm nor deny." Sally's chin nodded the tiniest bit.

That was what Preston George had been up to with Khaki. Were the women working at his company women who'd escaped abuse?

I clinked my coffee cup into its saucer. "That means that—"

"Isn't that Pete Brewer?"

I looked up. Pete Brewer was staring in our direction. I waved.

Sally shifted in her seat. "About your cousin Cora."

I'd forgotten all about poor Cora. "What do you require as a retainer? I brought my checkbook."

Sally suggested an amount.

It seemed very reasonable. "Done. I'll write you a check before we leave. Now about Khaki—"

"I'll tell you what I can, Mrs. Russell, but perhaps we could find a more discreet place to talk."

She was right. Half the people in the dining room were probably trying to listen in.

"The club was a bad idea."

"On the contrary. My omelet is excellent."

"I have an appointment at noon. Otherwise I'd ask you back to the house. May I come by your office tomorrow?"

"That would be fine." She pushed away from the table. "Thank you for brunch."

I took one last sip of coffee and stood as well. "Thank you for joining me."

We stepped into the hall that led to the front door and those four cups of coffee came home to roost. "Sally, you'll have to excuse me. I'm going to visit the powder room before I leave."

"Of course. I'll see you tomorrow."

Sally walked out into the cold, and I headed for the ladies' lounge. In the summertime, its I-wish-I-was-in-Nantucket-themed décor was odd enough. We were, after all, in Missouri, not Cape Cod. When the weather turned cold, all that white made the lounge feel like the inside of a freezer. I shivered when I entered.

I shivered again when Mary Beth appeared immediately after I did. Maybe because her husband's scowl had lingered.

She offered me a tentative smile. "Good morning."

"Good morning." I touched up my lipstick.

"I didn't know you knew Sally Broome."

"I don't really. I had a legal question."

"You?"

I nodded. "Me." I wasn't about to discuss Cora's problems with anyone at the club. "Say, I have a question for you, Mary Beth."

She tilted her chin. "What?"

"Khaki White worked for you, didn't she?"

"She did."

"Did you feel like her prices were fair?"

"Khaki's prices?" Her voice rose and she rubbed her throat. "Sorry. With this crazy weather, I'm coming down with a cold. Khaki's prices were right in line with the other decorators I talked to." She patted her hair and admired her reflection in the mirror.

"Really?"

"Really." She turned and faced me. "Why do you ask?"

No way was I going to explain that I suspected my cousin of murder. "No real reason." I scratched my nose.

She smiled at me in the mirror.

At least one of us was lying.

The drive home from the club was short—a good thing since my attention wasn't on the road. Already I was mapping a strategy for telling Anarchy that Mother's favorite cousin was probably a killer.

I parked in the circle drive in front of the house and hurried inside.

"Grace?" I called up the stairs "I'm home."

No answer. Well, not if I didn't count the sound of a door slamming. Apparently I was still on the no-talk list.

I hung up my coat and turned my attention to Max. "You're glad to see me, aren't you?"

He wagged his stubby tail and rubbed his head against the fabric of my suit.

"Let's get you a biscuit."

Max devoured his treat like a dog who hadn't seen food in a week then scratched on the back door.

I let him out and closed the door against a cold wind forcing its way into the house.

If ever there was a day for a fire in the hearth, this was it.

I hurried into the living room, turned the key on the gas starter in the fireplace, and held a long match under the logs waiting for a flame. The twisted newspaper stuffed in among the logs caught and burned brightly.

*Ding dong.*

I glanced out the front window. A white Mercedes was parked in the drive. Hunter's.

Just perfect. I glanced at my watch. The dial stood at 11:50.

Ten minutes till Anarchy arrived.

Hunter and Anarchy were like Champagne and beer. Fine on their own. A disaster together. Could I get rid of Hunter in ten minutes?

I hurried into the front hall and closed my fingers around the door knob.

Three things popped into my head in rapid succession. Hunter had too much pride to just show up at my house unannounced. Neither Cora nor Thornton drove a white Mercedes. And Khaki and Stan's killer was on the other side of the door. Unfortunately, my hand turned the knob before the last realization hit.

# TWENTY-TWO

Time slowed to a standstill. I threw my weight against the front door, hoping to close it before the man on the other side gained entry to my home.

I wasn't fast enough or heavy enough.

The door flew open and I stumbled backward.

Pete Brewer rushed into the foyer and slammed the door behind him.

Pete?

This wasn't the affable Pete I knew—the one I'd suspected of cheating on his wife. This Pete's face was suffused with rage. I might not have recognized him were he not wearing the same suit and tie he'd had on at the club.

This Pete pulled a gun from his coat pocket and pointed it at me. "You just couldn't leave well enough alone, could you?"

I didn't answer. I couldn't. I was too terrified. There was a man waving a gun in the foyer and Grace was upstairs.

I held up my hands, fingers spread wide, and found my voice. "Pete, please, calm down. Let's talk about this."

"What kind of fool do you think I am?"

Apparently the kind that threatened women with a .22.

"I don't think you're a fool. Please, put the gun down."

Anarchy would be here soon. Please, let him be on time. Better yet, early.

"Please, Pete. Put the gun down."

"You had to go sticking your nose where it didn't belong."

I hadn't stuck my nose anywhere near Pete's business. Not even close. But there was still a gun in my face. "I don't understand. Why are you doing this?"

"You know what I did. Mary Beth said you were asking about Khaki's fees." He waved the gun. "You were at brunch with that bitch lawyer." The color of his skin went from tomato to brick red. "I hate that bitch."

I clasped my hands together as if in prayer—*please don't shoot me*—and thought. Thought hard. I'd been so wrong. Not Thornton. Pete.

Playing dumb seemed the best plan. "You're angry because I had brunch with Sally Broome?"

"Don't. Say Her. Name!" Pete used the gun for emphasis, thrusting the muzzle at me with each syllable.

"Okay, okay. I'm sorry. I won't."

"And don't play stupid. I know you figured it out."

"Figured what out?" If I could just keep him talking...My voice was patient and sympathetic. Or at least I hoped it was. Hard to tell with all the blood roaring in my ears.

"You know I killed Khaki. You asked my wife about her fees."

Telling him that he was an idiot, that I hadn't suspected a thing until he pointed a gun in my face, didn't seem like much of a plan.

His face resembled one of those Greek masks—comedy, tragedy, mind-bending rage. He fisted his free hand. "I fell for her con. She was the best decorator in town." His voice pitched higher as if he were imitating Mary Beth. "She had to be. She charged the most. What a load of malarkey."

My fingers were colder than icicles, but I spread them wide and held them in front of me, pleading. "I don't know what you're talking about."

"You do. Stop lying. I hate liars."

An enraged man with a gun wanted me to admit to knowing he'd killed my decorator? Fine. "How did you find out what

Khaki was doing?" Surely at least five minutes had passed. I just had to keep him talking a little longer, until Anarchy arrived.

"Dan Fleming's accountant wanted to know why he'd paid so much for a china cabinet. I started looking at my bills. I even called an antiques appraiser." The gun in his hand shook. "Mary Beth is *my* wife. She doesn't get to leave, and she sure as hell doesn't get to steal from me."

"Mary Beth doesn't want to leave you." Soothing, that's the tone I was going for. "She said you were working things out."

A bead of sweat trickled from his hairline to his jawline. He grabbed his wrist with his free hand and steadied the gun. Too bad it was pointed at me. "I told Dan what I'd learned on Thursday night."

And now Dan's ex-wife was near death in the hospital.

My heart, which was already beating too fast, doubled its rate.

"I told Mary Beth what would happen."

"What?" My voice was faint. Not so soothing now.

"If she leaves me—if she tries to leave me—I'll kill her."

"She's not leaving." Was that a sound from the second floor? I didn't dare glance at the stairs. What if Pete guessed we weren't alone? "Please, Pete, let's sit down. You look as if you could use a drink." He didn't move. "May I get you a drink?"

Getting him away from the foyer—away from Grace—became my top priority. "I just lit a fire in the fireplace." Because we needed the right ambiance for him to shoot me. I side-stepped toward the living room with my heart in my throat.

Pete pursed his lips. Trying to figure out what I was up to? "Fine. I could use a scotch."

I hurried into the living room, the skin between my shoulder blades prickling, waiting for a *bang* and the tear of a bullet through my body.

I picked up a bottle, but my hands shook too much to pour. I clutched the edge of the drinks cart with my left hand, drew breath deep into my lungs, and steadied the hand holding the bottle. Would he notice if I looked at my watch? Would Anarchy get here in time?

I poured scotch into a glass and held it out to Pete.

He took the glass and drank.

"I'm not a bad guy."

Call me crazy, but in my book, killing two people made one a bad guy. I edged toward the fireplace where the poker was calling my name.

"Sit." He used the gun as a pointer. He wanted me in one of the wingback chairs.

I sat. Too far from the fireplace. Whacking him with a poker was not in my future.

"I didn't plan this. You weren't supposed to be involved."

That was patently ridiculous. He'd killed two people in my home. But I wasn't about to disagree—not when he was talking, not when noon and Anarchy's arrival grew closer by the second.

"None of this would have happened if Mary Beth had done what I told her."

Right. It was Mary Beth's fault. Two murders. Hopefully not three.

"What did you tell her to do?"

"What didn't I tell her? Dinner served late. The house never clean enough. She kept seeing Karen Fleming behind my back."

Those were his complaints? His justification for murder?

Pete drained his glass. "I took her to a club I belong to and she embarrassed me."

"A club?" I squeaked. Club K? It was Pete who had dropped the matchbook into the umbrella stand. I clutched the arm of the chair and lowered my voice to a range that humans could actually hear. "Would you like another scotch?"

"Don't you move." He crossed to the drinks cart and filled the old-fashioned glass to the rim.

I snuck a look at my watch. Four minutes till noon. Those four minutes stretched in front of me like a road without end.

"What about Stan?"

Pete looked up from his scotch and for an instant something like regret danced across his face. "I went back for more curry."

That wasn't much of an explanation.

Pete swirled the liquid in his glass and we both watched the scotch reflect the fire.

"If he'd controlled his wife, she wouldn't have been out stealing money from hard-working men. I told him as much."

"And he accused you of murder?"

Pete drank again. "He said something about Khaki and all the women she helped and I could tell. He knew I'd killed her. If I let him live, he'd have turned me in."

So he'd thwhacked poor Stan over the head with a candlestick.

Now I was the one who knew Pete was a killer. He'd come here to kill me.

*Click-click-click-click.*

"What's that?" Pete demanded.

That was Max's in-need-of-a-trim nails on the hardwood. "Max." My lips were numb. Unless Max had grown opposable thumbs (possible, but highly unlikely), Grace had let him in. Oh dear Lord.

Max bounded into the living room and stopped short. Who could blame him? Anger and fear were as real and palpable as the people in the room. The dog cocked his head to the side and stared at Pete.

Max knew Pete. Back when Max was a puppy, Henry deluded himself into believing that Max could be a hunting dog. Max, who was more a do-what-I-want-when-I-want kind of dog, disabused Henry of the idea after one three-day hunting trip at Pete's hunting lodge.

Now Max growled. Deep in his throat. A ridge of hair rose on his back.

"Max!" I wouldn't be able to stand it if Pete shot Max. Where was Anarchy?

"Tell him to sit." The gun tracked between me and my dog.

"Max. Come."

Max considered my proposition and rejected it. He growled and showed Pete his teeth.

"I don't want to hurt the dog. Call him off."

"Max!" A note of hysteria crept into my voice.

My dog turned and looked at me, his expression clear. He had this handled if I'd just shut up.

"There you are, Mom." Grace stood in the doorway to the front hall with half a laundry basket's worth of clothes draped over her arm "How do I wash these?" While it was true, Grace didn't have the slightest clue how to do laundry, it was also true she didn't need to. Aggie handled the laundry. "Warm or cold?" she insisted.

I couldn't answer and not because I didn't know that navy and black tee shirts should be washed on cold. Fear rendered me mute.

What was she thinking? She could have run straight out the back door. Been safe. Instead, she was making this harebrained attempt to save me. With laundry.

"Hi, Mr. Brewer." Did Grace not notice the gun in his hand? "Seriously, Mom. Warm or cold? Will you come help me?"

Did she really think Pete would let me—us—step out of the room to do a load of laundry?

"I wish you hadn't come in here, Grace." Pete sounded sincere. "I wish you weren't home."

Now Grace's gaze landed on the gun. "You wanted me to come home and find my mother dead? You wanted to make me an orphan?"

Her questions hung in the air, too painful, too real.

"I'm sorry." Pete lifted the gun.

Oh my God! Not Grace. "Max!" Something in my voice told the dog that now was the time. He lunged.

*Bang!*

The sound of the gun discharging pushed everything else out of the room. Pushed the air out of my lungs.

Grace!

I turned. My daughter stood straight and tall and perfect next to the door.

It was Pete who dropped to the floor. Pete and his scotch and his gun. He fell too close to the damned gun.

Pete's hand scrabbled across the carpet, reaching.

With a growl worthy of a hellhound, Max's teeth closed on his wrist.

*Crash!* The sound of a door being kicked in carried from the foyer.

"Ellison!" Anarchy raced into the living room with his gun drawn. His gaze took in Pete and Max on the floor.

Max yanked on Pete's wrist.

Pete yowled. "Get him off me!"

Grace stumbled then. She leaned against the wall, her eyes as wide as saucers and her lips pulled back from her teeth.

The poor child looked horrified. And no wonder. The collection of tee shirts draped over her arm had slipped to the floor revealing a gun. My gun. She'd shot Pete.

With his own gun, a .38, pointed at Pete, Anarchy picked up the dainty but deadly .22 off the floor. "Call off the dog, Ellison."

"Max, let go."

For once, Max listened to me. He released Pete, stalked over to me, and sat next to my chair. "Good dog." I scratched behind his ears and tried not to notice Pete's blood on his jowls.

Anarchy approached Grace and gently pried my .22 from her shaking hand.

"What happened?"

Anarchy leveled his cop gaze on me.

"Pete killed Khaki. And Stan. And he came here to kill me." I was grateful to be sitting. My knees weren't up to the job of holding me upright. I turned and smiled at my daughter (my lips curled up but the expression felt like a grimace). "Grace shot him."

"And what's your version, Grace?"

"I heard the front door slam and then voices. When I peeked downstairs, I saw Mr. Brewer with a gun."

So, rather than escaping the house, she'd fetched my gun? "Gra—"

Anarchy held up a hand, stopping me. "Let her finish, Ellison."

"I called the police, but I was worried they wouldn't get here in time. I got Mom's gun out of her bedside table and covered it with some laundry." She looked down at the pile of darks on the floor and swallowed audibly.

"You know how to shoot?"

She nodded. "My dad taught me."

"Is this the first time you've shot a person?" Anarchy's voice was as gentle as I'd ever heard it.

Something between a sob and a laugh broke free of her lips and her whole body shook as if she was having a small seizure.

"Grace, you need to sit down." Anarchy led her to the couch. "You saved your mom, Grace. Remember that."

Over the objection of my shaky knees, I hauled myself out of the chair, stumbled across the living room, and joined her on the couch. We wrapped our arms around each other. Nothing had ever smelled as sweet as the scent of her apple blossom shampoo. I stroked her hair. "You should have run."

"And let him shoot you?" She sniffled and wiped her eyes.

"Anarchy was on his way."

"I didn't know that."

Was this how Mother felt about me? A rush of love coupled with a desire to wring my neck? "You could have been shot."

"I wasn't."

"Be that as it may—"

"Mom." She made one syllable into three.

"Don't do it again."

She snorted.

"And you're ungrounded."

That earned me another squeeze. I squeezed back. The girl

in my arms was so precious. If something happened to her...I swallowed a lump in my throat. "I love you, Grace."

"I love you, too."

Max whined softly. He wanted in on the love-fest.

Grace let go of me and wrapped her arms around his neck. "You are the bravest, best dog ever."

She shouldn't say things like that. They'd go straight to his head.

I turned toward Anarchy. He'd been busy while Grace and I talked. He'd hauled Pete, whose right shoulder was now crimson, off the floor. The man who'd come to my house to kill me wore handcuffs and the enraged expression that had transformed his face was gone, replaced by confusion—as if the turn of events was too much for him to process.

"It wasn't my fault," he said. "I had to do it."

My fingers stiffened. They curved into claws. My teeth clenched. My tenuous hold on my emotions slipped. "Bullshit."

Next to me, Grace's jaw dropped.

"You killed two people. Good people. You didn't have to do that. You planned on killing me—" I reached out and took Grace's hand "—and Grace. You didn't have to do that. And why? Because the wife you hit wanted to leave you?" My spine locked into perfect posture mode. "You are pathetic."

"Ellison—"

I held up my free hand. Anarchy would not interrupt me. "There will come a day when society knows exactly what to do with men like you." I knew now, but society probably wouldn't approve of forced castration. "You're going to prison, and I hope to God they throw away the key."

"Go, Mom."

The rage had returned to Pete's face.

"I should have shot you the minute I walked through the door."

"Your mistake."

"Ellison, would you please call the precinct? I need backup."

I recognized a diversion technique when I saw it. If Anarchy thought for one minute that—

"I'll do it, Detective Jones." Grace released my hand and stood.

*No!* I wanted her on the couch, next to me—I wasn't ready to let go.

She hurried out of the room—a young woman who neither wanted nor needed her mother to worry about her.

I watched her go with an aching heart.

"Ahem."

I turned and faced Anarchy.

"What exactly was it you wanted to tell me?"

# TWENTY-THREE

The hospital coffee shop was fast becoming as familiar to me as my own kitchen.

I sat in a booth next to the window where Monday morning sunshine—weak, but there—gilded my coffee cup.

Mother sat across the table. She was not happy. "He held you at gunpoint?"

"We've been over this twice." Three times, but who was counting?

"Do you realize what this does to my nerves?"

"Actually, I do." I understood exactly the horrible knowledge that one couldn't protect one's daughter from darkness or evil or pain. I reached across the table and took her hand. "It's over now."

She stared down at our two hands. "For now."

"I promise. No more bodies."

Mother squeezed my fingers but shook her head. "You can't make that promise. You find bodies everywhere. It's as if you've been cursed."

She spoke from a place of worry. Remembering that—remembering how worried I'd been for Grace—kept me from snatching my hand away. I cleared my throat and sent the conversation in a new direction. "I haven't been up to see Cora yet. How is she?" My morning thus far had consisted of helping Preston load a cranky Jinx into his car. He'd been infinitely patient and loving and had tucked Jinx into the passenger seat like precious cargo.

With her safely strapped in, Preston turned and dropped a kiss on my cold cheek. "Thank you."

"You're welcome." I glanced at Jinx in the car. "You know, you could have told her about what Khaki was doing." He could have told me.

"What Khaki was doing was illegal—" he smiled at his wife who was ignoring us and fiddling with the radio "—and Jinx can't keep a secret."

I didn't argue. Instead, I tapped on the passenger window, waved a last goodbye to Jinx, and re-entered the hospital, where I met Mother for coffee.

One of Mother's perfectly manicured fingers tapped the back of my hand. "Cora is divorcing Thornton." She sounded resigned, not scandalized.

I raised my brows.

"Don't look surprised. It's about time she stood up to him."

I wasn't surprised Cora was divorcing Thornton. I was surprised Mother wasn't having a faunching fit over a divorce in the family.

"People accord you exactly the amount of respect you accord yourself. Cora finally realized that."

Mother made it sound so easy.

Her grip on my hand tightened. "What's happening with you and Hunter?"

"Nothing."

Her diamond ring dug into my fingers. "Nothing?"

"I told him I'm not ready for a relationship."

Mother sighed. I'd disappointed her again. "Just because you've spent the week around bad husbands—"

"It's not that."

"Then what?"

Anarchy Jones. But I wasn't about to tell her that. "I'm not ready. Henry hasn't been dead six months."

Her lips pursed as if she'd bitten into a sour pickle and she tsked.

I stood. "I'm going to visit Karen Fleming."

Mother patted her lips with a paper napkin she pulled from the silver dispenser on the table. "Don't worry about Hunter, Ellison. I'll smooth things over."

"I don't want you to—"

She waved away my objections. "Give Karen my regards."

I couldn't control what Mother did any more than I could control Grace. Then again, Mother couldn't control me.

Karen's hospital bed was cranked somewhere between sitting and reclining. Her face was still swollen, still purple. If anything, she looked worse than she had when I found her. She opened her eyes, saw me, and somehow she managed a smile.

"How are you feeling?" I asked.

"Like hell." The smile remained on her lips. "If hell were at the top of the world."

Dan had been arrested and charged with attempted murder. That was thanks to Anarchy and a call from Daddy to the police commissioner. Peters had wanted to charge Dan Fleming with breaking and entering.

"You saved my life."

"Mary Beth would have found you."

"True, but I don't know if she would have called for help."

"She would have. You're her friend."

"Maybe." Karen glanced down at the bed. "You don't know what it's like to live in fear of your husband. She wasn't supposed to be there." Karen smoothed the top sheet. "I heard Pete tried to kill you."

"Yes."

"And he killed Khaki and Stan."

I nodded. "Yes."

"Because Khaki was giving hopeless women hope. A way out."

"Yes. But he won't harm anyone else. Ever."

We visited for a few more minutes, then I said goodbye.

I paused outside Karen's room and leaned against a wall the color of old oatmeal. One of the fluorescent bulbs in the overhead lights needed changing—an annoying buzz mixed with the distant sound of nurses voices.

Poor Karen. Poor Mary Beth. Poor Cora.

I shook my head. Had the past week taught me nothing? They weren't objects of pity. They were survivors.

The sound of steps on the tile floor brought me out of my reverie. Anarchy Jones walked toward me, purpose evident in every stride.

He stopped when he saw me. "Ellison."

"Anarchy."

And just like that, we ran out of things to say.

All the things I ought to tell him ran through my head. *Thank you* being chief among them. They were followed quickly by the things I'd never say—*dear God, you're handsome.*

Anarchy smiled—the kind of smile that made me wonder if he could read my mind—leaned forward, and brushed his lips against my cheek—the softest of kisses.

It set the nerve endings in my cheek on fire.

"Are you free for dinner tonight?" His voice was velvety and seductive and beguiling.

I caught my lip in my teeth, looked up at the ceiling, looked down at the floor, and gave him my answer.

# AUTHOR'S NOTE

In the early 1970s, spousal abuse was deemed a private matter by both the police and the medical community. Authorities were reluctant to intervene in matters between a husband and a wife. As such, I have pushed the envelope by creating Phoenix House. In fact, the first domestic violence shelter did not open in Missouri until 1976.

JULIE MULHERN

Julie Mulhern is the *USA Today* bestselling author of The Country Club Murders. She is a Kansas City native who grew up on a steady diet of Agatha Christie. She spends her spare time whipping up gourmet meals for her family, working out at the gym and finding new ways to keep her house spotlessly clean—and she's got an active imagination. Truth is—she's an expert at calling for take-out, she grumbles about walking the dog and the dust bunnies under the bed have grown into dust lions.

**Henery Press Mystery Books**

And finally, before you go...
Here are a few other mysteries
you might enjoy:

# NUN TOO SOON

Alice Loweecey

## A Giulia Driscoll Mystery (#1)

Giulia Falcone-Driscoll has just taken on her first impossible client: The Silk Tie Killer. He's hired Driscoll Investigations to prove his innocence and they have only thirteen days to accomplish it. Talk about being tried in the media. Everyone in town is sure Roger Fitch strangled his girlfriend with one of his silk neckties. And then there's the local TMZ wannabes stalking Giulia and her client for sleazy sound bites.

On top of all that, her assistant's first baby is due any second, her scary smart admin still doesn't relate well to humans, and her police detective husband insists her client is guilty. About this marriage thing—it's unknown territory, but it sure beats ten years of living with 150 nuns.

Giulia's ownership of Driscoll Investigations hasn't changed her passion for justice from her convent years. But the more dirt she digs up, the more she's worried her efforts will help a murderer escape. As the client accuses DI of dragging its heels on purpose, Giulia thinks The Silk Tie Killer might be choosing one of his ties for her own neck.

Available at booksellers nationwide and online

Visit www.henerypress.com for details

# CIRCLE OF INFLUENCE

Annette Dashofy

## A Zoe Chambers Mystery (#1)

Zoe Chambers, paramedic and deputy coroner in rural Pennsylvania's tight-knit Vance Township, has been privy to a number of local secrets over the years, some of them her own. But secrets become explosive when a dead body is found in the Township Board President's abandoned car.

As a January blizzard rages, Zoe and Police Chief Pete Adams launch a desperate search for the killer, even if it means uncovering secrets that could not only destroy Zoe and Pete, but also those closest to them.

Available at booksellers nationwide and online

Visit www.henerypress.com for details

# TELL ME NO LIES

Lynn Chandler Willis

## An Ava Logan Mystery (#1)

Ava Logan, single mother and small business owner, lives deep in the heart of the Appalachian Mountains, where poverty and pride reign. As publisher of the town newspaper, she's busy balancing election season stories and a rash of ginseng thieves.

And then the story gets personal. After her friend is murdered, Ava digs for the truth all the while juggling her two teenage children, her friend's orphaned toddler, and her own muddied past. Faced with threats against those closest to her, Ava must find the killer before she, or someone she loves, ends up dead.

Available at booksellers nationwide and online

Visit www.henerypress.com for details

Printed in Great Britain
by Amazon